JILLEEN
DOLBEARE

Splintered
Secret

VINCI

BOOKS

By Jilleen Dolbeare

Splintered Magic

Splintered Magic
Splintered Veil
Splintered Fate
Splintered Haven
Splintered Secret
Splintered Destiny

Vinci Books

vinci-books.com

Published by Vinci Books Ltd in 2025

1

A CIP catalogue record for this book is available from the British Library.
Paperback ISBN: 9781036706111

Chapter One

It wasn't much of a party after the cops hauled Megan off in cuffs. I looked helplessly at my friends. The Whelans were holding Luke back. Anything he did now would just add to our problems. The vamps apparently had the cops in their pocket. We watched them go in stunned silence. They had nothing to hold Megan on, nothing. She'd been in the hospital or on her way home from it when the Blankenships were murdered.

A good lawyer and we'd have her out, I told myself. Now, to find a lawyer.

"Anyone know a lawyer?" I asked. I wrapped my arms around myself and shivered. Gabe pulled me to him, but even his presence wasn't calming the ache in my heart and the pit in my stomach.

"Why didn't they arrest me or Luke?" I asked. We'd been the ones that called in the body. We'd been on the scene and were the most likely suspects.

"Because she's the most vulnerable," Noah growled.

I closed my eyes. He was right. The vampires would

have a hard time with all of us, we were supernaturals. But Megan? For all her fierceness and mental fortitude, she was human. They could manipulate her in a million ways. I felt sick. Even Mr. Mittens couldn't protect me from this. I'd have to figure this one out without relying on him to fix it by eating someone.

I wondered if the gargoyles knew a lawyer. They seemed to be up on all the vampire tricks, maybe they had experience with this one. Yes, I'd go inside and find Sam's phone number.

I left everyone to clean up, all the eating and happy banter forgotten. We'd save it. We'd spring Megan today, and hopefully Bella wouldn't drink her dry. I looked Sam up in my system and dialed.

It rang three times.

"Brigid, how kind of you to call," Sam said.

"Thanks." I didn't wait or follow up with any other pleasantries, I just blurted out, "I need help."

There was a quiet beat. "I thought the vampires left?"

"Me too, but the cops just came and arrested Megan. When they did, Bella, Vic Constantine's enforcer, was with them."

"Hmmm. That is not good."

"No."

"What can I do to help?" he asked, concern in his voice.

"Do you know a lawyer? Someone up on vamp machinations?"

I could hear the phone muffle and some incoherent talking in the background. "Yes, Brigid, but getting them to you on time could be troublesome. They may be either drinking her for information, or worse. This needs to be handled immediately."

I knew that. I wanted to do something now, that's why I'd called.

"Where are you?"

"I'm at currently home. I could be there in three hours. But that might be too late."

"If you can get here, I can take us back, like I did before."

"Ah, yes." He was quiet for a minute, probably thinking. "Let me gather a few of my brethren, and I'll be there as soon as I can."

"Thank you, thank you so much! I owe you!" I said, the tears clogging my voice.

"It's my purpose. I have no need for thanks." He hung up.

Everyone was waiting for news in the kitchen. They'd allowed me some privacy so I could make my phone call in peace.

Luke couldn't wait. "What did he say?"

I looked up at him and wiped my face. "They're coming."

"They?" he demanded.

"Yes, he's coming and bringing a few other gargoyles. They should be here in three or four hours."

"Hours?" He scrubbed his hands through his hair.

"I can time walk them when they get here. We have options. We need to use our time to think our way out of this so we can help her."

"That's it!" Luke exclaimed. "Time walk back and hide her from the cops!"

I froze. Was it that simple? "I..." I thought it through, then sighed. That wouldn't work. I didn't even know how close I could get to myself by duplicating myself in time. Also, the cops knew where she lived. If they didn't come now, they'd come another time, and wouldn't stop. We had to deal with the issue now.

I explained my reasoning.

Luke took a deep breath and let his family calm him. Gabe was attempting the same with me, his hand on my back, rubbing and scratching.

I gestured for everyone to take a seat. Chef Jack already had the food from the barbecue put away. We'd all thought we'd have a hundred years before we had to deal with the vamps again this soon after defeating them since it took that long to have a vampire strong enough to be worth anything to Vic. This was shaking us all to our foundations. The vamps were a nearly impossible foe. Without the gargoyles, we'd have been soundly defeated.

This time, I wasn't going to wait to call for help. The gargoyles were coming, and I wanted more fireballs from Dana. I excused myself, went to my room, and took the communication ball from my underwear drawer. Concentrating on it, I held it in my hand until it flashed and vibrated. I returned it to the drawer. Unfortunately, I couldn't make anyone answer. Dana would come when she felt like it.

I'd done all I could, short of storming the police station, power blazing. But that was a last resort. I had to believe that the police in town were human, probably being manipulated or bribed. Hopefully, it was that—normal non-magical issues. However, there was Bella...

When I returned to the kitchen, Noah and Izzy were gone. I looked at Madison for an explanation.

"We didn't know if the cops would go to the police station for sure. They chased after the cars. I just hope we didn't think about it too late."

Me too. I hadn't even thought of it. It was times like this

I wished I had the power of flight, so we could follow them better. Invisibility didn't help if you didn't know where anyone was. If the vamps had the police in their pockets, they could go anywhere. That thought caused chills. I shivered until my teeth clacked together. I considered asking Brightfeather for a flight to follow, but she had her eggs to watch over and shouldn't leave them for long.

Gabe pulled me in close, and I looked around for my cat. "Where did Mr. Mittens go?"

No one remembered seeing him leave. I needed him, but he was his own creature, and I didn't truly own him. Not that you could own any kind of cat.

I pulled away from Gabe and looked out the door just in case. But Mr. Mittens wasn't in sight. Even if he couldn't help, I needed his comfort. I called to him silently.

"Mr. Mittens, where are you?"

I'm hunting a bloodsucker, was his terse answer.

The anger and hurt welled up in me. I wanted to be there with him, to make it pay, but if he could bring it back, we could get answers.

"Catch it and bring it to me," I demanded.

I intend to.

"Mr. Mittens is hunting a vamp in my woods. He'll bring it here if he catches it," I announced.

Luke growled, and the hair on the back of my neck rose. He could be scary.

"We'll find her, and we'll get her back," I said with conviction. I wasn't going to believe anything different. I would get her back, and vampires were going to die.

Got him! Mr. Mittens triumphant yowl screamed through my mind.

"He's got one, he's bringing it back."

I felt a pulse of magic, and my cat, in his true form,

appeared from the ether, dragging a male vamp, its shoulder caught in his teeth. Mr. Mittens had realm walked them.

I wasn't sure how we were going to contain an old vamp. It had to be old to be out in the sun, even in the shade. But it looked scared, if such beings even felt fear.

I called a bright sphere of light to my hand and held it near the vamp's face.

"If you move, even a finger, I'll fry you. Understand?"

"Yes." It glared at me.

"Release him, please," I asked my cat.

The vamp hit the floor with a thump. It held still, so I knew it believed me.

"You may sit in the chair." I nodded at Madison, and she dragged a chair over to the wall. The vamp got up and sat in it, while Mr. Mittens stood, ready to pounce.

The vamp squinted in the face of my light ball, so I squelched it. I stayed a short distance away, so I could react if it decided to try and take me out, even though Mr. Mittens was close enough to stop it.

"Where did you take my friend?" I asked.

It snarled at me. "I can't tell you."

"If you can't, you are no use to us, and there will be no future for you." My voice rang ice cold, which surprised me, but this was a monster, not a human, not even something with compassion.

"He'll kill me."

"*I* will kill you now. If you cooperate with me, you'll at least have a chance."

He grew quiet, but his face showed his thought process as it distorted and stilled.

"He has a small yacht. It's in the bay. He'll leave at slack tide. If you want your friend, it will have to be then."

I looked at Luke, but he was already dialing.

Madison said, "I'm looking it up."

I nodded.

"Noah," Luke said. "They're heading for the bay." Silence. "They're going to put her on a yacht. Shouldn't be hard to find." He turned to us. "What's the name of the yacht?"

I didn't think that was important. I didn't know that there were many yachts that accessed the bay, but who knew.

"What's the name of the yacht?" I demanded.

"The Silver Sipper."

"Did you hear that, Luke?"

"Yeah, got it." He relayed the info to Noah and hung up.

"What does he want from her?" I asked the vamp.

He cocked his head at me. Then shrugged. "How would I know?"

I felt my lip curl. I hated these creatures, and I didn't feel nice. I summoned a stream of fire and sent it to the creature's arm.

He shrieked in pain.

I cut off the fire before the whole creature went up.

"He'll turn her and use her against you!" he screamed.

My blood ran cold. Damn them.

I wanted the creature gone before I sent it up in flames. I gestured to Gabe to open the kitchen door. Once Gabe was out of reach, I nodded at Mr. Mittens, who backed up. "Go," I said to the creature. The vamp was gone in an instant. Gabe closed the door.

The second the gargoyles arrived, we were going to destroy the vamps at the dock, and we had to be ready.

"Get your weapons," I said. "We're going vamp hunting."

Chapter Two

The Whelans left to prepare, leaving me, Gabe, and my cat. I didn't know what to do. I could time walk three or four people, but not all of them. It was too exhausting. Mr. Mittens could take care of himself, but I had Luke, Madison, Gabe, and the gargoyles. I needed help. I guess I could take a group, come back and rest, then take the second group. Time travel messed with my head. Still, it would be easier with another time traveler.

I went and changed into something I could fight in. Gabe was already in jeans and athletic shoes. Since we hadn't gotten to eat before everything went down, I forced us to eat something, so we'd have the energy we needed. Jim and Chef Jack left to meet up with Noah at Tillamook Bay, so at least they'd be close in time and space when we needed them. The bay was thirty minutes away, and the cops had five to seven minutes on Noah and Izzy. Although, I had no idea how fast Noah was driving.

I wasn't sure how many gargoyles were coming, but I had

at least two werewolves and Gabe to transport. The most I'd done so far had been four. I could maybe take one more and still have some energy. I wasn't sure about more than that.

If I did two groups in a row? I wasn't sure I'd have anything left to fight with. My magic was exhilarating, but it had limits. And time walking was it. If we were fighting in Faerie or here on my land, it would be easier, and I'd recover faster. Probably something else the vamps had learned when they'd drank from Megan the first time. They knew everything she knew.

They thought their numbers and savagery would overwhelm us before, and they'd been wrong. Now, they were going to play it safe. Well, they didn't know I'd be bringing gargoyles again. It had still been day when they'd taken Megan, even if it was on the verge of night. So, they knew we didn't have gargoyle guests at our shindig.

Hopefully, my time walking wasn't in the forefront of their thoughts.

There was a sudden flash of light, and I blinked. Dana had arrived. She looked at me with a sneer. "What trouble have you gotten into now?"

I sighed. "The same one—vampires."

She cocked her horsey head. "It's a good thing I've been stocking up on these." She thrust her arm out with a large bag dangling from her hand.

"Are those...?"

"Of course, they are," she snipped.

She looked as though she were going to realm walk away. "Wait!" I yelled a little louder than I intended.

She crossed her arms and tapped a hoof on my myrtle wood floor. "What is it?"

She owed me nothing, but I needed help even if that

would only put me further in her debt. When it was time for payback, I'd be doomed.

"The vamps have taken Megan. I need to time walk a group larger than I can at once. I was hoping you could help me?"

"Hmmm." She pinched her mouth together, and her large nostrils flared. She liked Megan, but she wasn't that happy about helping me. Though, I was hoping she would for Megan.

"That isn't my skill to offer."

"What?" She'd taught me to time walk. I'd assumed it was one of her powers.

"I use a magic ball. I don't have any to spare, and whoever uses them must be able to realm walk first."

A wave of despair staggered me. I'd half hoped she'd be the answer to my problem. She frowned at me. The only other realm walker I knew besides Mr. Mittens was Goch, and I didn't know where he was currently. Plus, I'd have to teach him to time walk *if* Dana would even give me a ball for that.

"I'll see if your grandfather can spare a moment."

I looked at her in shock. The last time I'd asked, she'd said he was too busy, and I believed her. When we'd left Faerie, everything was in disarray. There'd been an attempted coup, and my grandfather was the clean-up crew.

"He's free?" I asked.

She shrugged. "Perhaps."

That would be an amazing boon. Not only was he gifted with thirteen elements like I was, he'd been using them for centuries. I was a novice, while he was a power to be reckoned with.

"Don't get your hopes up." She flashed away.

Right. If he didn't come, I'd be even more lost to despair. I had to plan as though I were doing this alone. I felt sick. The stress of getting there on time with the people I needed was immense.

The only thing I could do was to take one group, recover a few hours at the waterfall, then take the next. That would be the plan. I pushed down my anxiety by reassuring myself I had time as long as I had time magic. I rushed back to the kitchen to tell Gabe and hand him Dana's fire balls.

Gabe and Mr. Mittens were both in the kitchen. Mr. Mittens was cleaning up his supper, and Gabe was drinking a glass of water.

I thrust out the bag of balls. "Dana came through! Also, she might be able to get my grandfather to help," I gushed.

Mr. Mittens blinked. *Are you sure, pet?*

I shrugged. "No, but there's a chance."

"How many balls did she bring?" Gabe asked, more practical than either of us.

"She didn't say, but that bag is much larger than the last one. Hopefully, a lot."

"Do you have any myrtle oil left?"

"Yes, it's under the sink. I think there's quite a bit." I walked over and rummaged under the sink, pulling out two gallon jugs. "This is what I have here. Jim has some at the stable."

We both stared at it. It slowed down the vamps slightly, but it had mostly been a disappointment. Basically, it just made them wipe off your skin before they bit you. We'd been hoping it poisoned them or drove them back like a cross in the movies did. Still, it was the only deterrent besides the high-powered flashlights we had.

Gabe had proven that his healing gift could "cure" the

vamps—turn them human again. That had been useful. Mr. Mittens could rip them apart, as could the werewolves. I could fry them with lightning and fire. The only issue was how fast the vampires were. We couldn't respond as quickly as they could, and that more than evened the fight.

Finally, when it seemed I couldn't wait a second longer, a car pulled into the driveway. The gargoyles were here. Gabe and I ran out the door.

Chapter Three

It had still been light when Megan had been taken. That would keep the young vampires away, but it was an issue for the gargoyles. So, if I walked the gargoyles back to that time, they wouldn't be able to shift into gargoyle form immediately. Which was something I'd been worrying about while we waited. I watched the sun anxiously.

Sam and three other gargoyles exited the car. I wanted to hug him. His smile was large and genuine, as was mine. He'd helped us when all seemed lost.

"Sam!" I waved.

"Brigid, I want you to meet my friends." He waved at the three others. "This is Brandon, George, and Felicity. Felicity is a lawyer."

I was so relieved. I didn't really think we'd need one, knowing that the vampires had kidnapped Megan rather than taking her to regular police lockup, but if we could get it all before a judge, maybe it would take away their advantage and remove the police from the equation in the future.

Felicity reached back into the car and pulled out a

leather satchel. 'I have documents to release Megan. There wasn't an official warrant issued, not that I could find anywhere. I've notified the FBI and the state police. If they don't release her, legally they don't have a leg to stand on. The local police have already received the documents.'

I was so grateful, I wanted to cry. But even if it wasn't legal, the vamps still had her. If we could stop the police cars before they reached the yacht, we might be able to convince them of their error. However, Bella being in the car made me think that the police were under her control. They might not be fully aware of what they were doing. That control was what we needed to end.

How? My mind magic would be the best bet, but I wasn't trained in it. I'd have to wing it. Plus, we'd have to overpower however many vamps were meeting the police cars when we got to the bay.

And I could only carry a few people back in time with me. I'd hoped my grandfather would show up before I had to make the decision.

"If I take you back in time with me," I said to Sam, "it'll still be light. You won't be able to shift."

He nodded. "Light is fine. There just can't be direct sunlight. If it's just twilight, we're golden. What time are we going back to?" We'd been going to eat at seven, but since I'd been talking to Brightfeather, it was later than that.

"Seven thirty?" I said uncertainly. I could picture the place the sun was in the sky, and it was low.

Sam nodded. "Sunset is at seven forty-three. As long as we wait those thirteen minutes, we'll be fine to shift."

"Is it sunlight hitting you, or the sun being up?" I asked, an idea formulating.

"Sunlight. We can be out in gargoyle form when it's

cloudy, but if a stray sunbeam breaks free, we turn to stone. If we're flying…"

I got it. They'd be nothing but dust. But I could change that. I had shadow magic. If I could block off enough area, the sun wouldn't touch them for those thirteen minutes. I didn't know how big an area I could affect, though. I stepped back, and although Sam was still talking to me, I wasn't paying attention. I called up my shadow magic. This time, instead of using it to conceal me, I cast it above us. It grew dark. Everyone looked up. I cast it in as large a space as I could. I covered my entire parking lot, which was half a square acre. A large space.

Everyone was silent, then Sam chuckled. "That would work."

I smiled and let the shadow dissipate. As long as there wasn't a big wind, I could even let it sit there without effort. Win-win.

"Now, we just need to make it to the dock before they do," I said. And everyone agreed with me. I looked around. I think I could take four others, maybe five. The first time I'd realm walked, I'd dragged Mr. Mittens, Megan, and Sofia with me into Faerie. So, I knew I could take three without effort. I'd taken four through time during the last battle with the vampires a few months ago. That hadn't been too much of a strain. I was confident I could take five. Mr. Mittens couldn't come, being off the property, but I would have to take Gabe and Luke with me for sure. Luke wouldn't want to be left behind, and Gabe's powers were too handy to leave behind. Plus, I wanted him with me. He steadied me, heart and soul.

That meant I could only take three gargoyles. "Sam, I can only bring three of you," I said without offering any more information.

"No problem. Felicity is a non-combatant."

I looked at the woman. I considered asking about that, since I still didn't know much about gargoyles except for a throwaway statement from Sam that gargoyles were created to destroy vampires. However, now wasn't the time. I stuffed that idea away.

I looked at Gabe. He held the bag of fireballs and looked ready to go. I was ready as well.

"No time like the present," Sam said when I looked at him with a question in my eyes.

"Yes, we should go."

I felt pressed for time, although I wasn't, but I was desperate to get Megan back from the creepy vampire that had taken her. Knowing that Vic Constantine waited to take vengeance on me by hurting or turning my friend filled me with white hot rage. We had to get there in time. We all grabbed hands, and I walked us to the practice planet. It hadn't been a strain at all. I gave a sigh of relief, then one more step to the dock at the same time Megan was being abducted at my house. I checked my phone. I'd done it. We were here and in time.

We scouted around the area. Sure enough, a very expensive-looking yacht floated just inside the mouth of the bay, waiting. No one appeared to be on deck. Someone should be here guarding the way to the dock. We were way at the end, so I didn't see guards, but they could be up by the entrance.

"Let's go find the guards," I whispered.

"We're going to look conspicuous if we all go together," Luke said. "Gabe and I will go have a look. The vamps seem to sense you gargoyles."

That was true. Somehow, the vamps had known when Sam had come to stay at my inn and had declared war on us because of it. Well, one of the reasons why. The other was that their leader, Vic Constantine, wanted this territory for himself and didn't want any competition from the other supernaturals that lived here. Namely me and the werewolves.

"Ok, we'll try to find the skiff that is going out to the yacht," I said.

Luke and Gabe strolled off, trying to blend in like they were coming home from a fishing trip, only without any gear or fish. Bad fishermen *do* exist.

Sam, the other two gargoyles, and I worked our way down the dock, checking each occupied slip for boats ready to go or containing vamps. Most boats were just sitting there, waiting for their owners. But a few were getting cleaned up or prepped for tomorrow. The second to last boat fit the bill. It had two men hanging around, and the one inside looked like he knew what he was doing. He wore Grunden bibs and smoked a cherry-scented cigarillo. His face was weathered, and he looked extremely bored. The other man was wearing a Kilchis police uniform and was acting as a guard. Neither were vamps. Still, this had to be the boat. It seemed that the yacht would stay anchored in the mouth of the bay after all.

I stopped, and the gargoyles did as well, recognizing the same thing I did. "This has to be it."

Sam agreed. The gargoyles spread out, acting like they were going to two other boats near the one we'd identified. I turned and headed towards the top of the dock where Luke and Gabe had gone. I had to let them know.

I checked my phone. The police would be here soon with Megan—five minutes or less. I ran. When I made it to the top, Luke was standing over the body of a man. My heart beat hard, was that Gabe? But no, Gabe was walking towards me, dragging another man by the elbow. The man was crying and stumbling, his hands over his face.

I reached Luke first. "What happened?"

"This one is human; I knocked him out."

I looked at him closely, another Kilchis police officer. The vamps did have them under their control. I nodded.

Gabe finally joined us. "This one is also human now."

That explained the weeping and stumbling. Gabe had cured him. Who knew how long he'd lived—or unlived?—before being turned back to human. Since vamps had to cook about a hundred years to be useful, this one could be several hundred years old. He'd have to relearn everything.

Gabe pushed him down to sit on a railing, and we all ignored him.

"That's all I saw," Gabe said.

"Me too," Luke added.

"There are two more humans at the boat, a fisherman, and another police officer," I added.

Luke smiled deviously. "I'm gonna impersonate an officer."

Chapter Four

Luke stripped the unconscious man and donned his clothing. They were a similar size, although Luke was a little broader through the shoulders and a tiny bit shorter. But Gabe was tall, so he couldn't pull it off, and I was way shorter, so that wouldn't work either. Once Luke was dressed, he said he'd stay and guard the dock. Gabe headed down to join the gargoyles, and I hid in my shadow magic next to the dock entrance. We waited.

After what seemed like forever but was in reality more like two minutes, the two police cars pulled up and parked. Their lights weren't on, and neither were the sirens. I texted Gabe. "They're here."

Two officers exited one car, and then another exited the second one. I recognized one of the cops—the woman—from the first time I'd met her when Luke and I discovered the body of my first guest.

Officer Lopez opened the back door of her patrol car, and Bella, Vic Constantine's enforcer, swung her legs out and exited the car. Then Bella reached back inside and pulled Megan out by the arm. Officer Lopez stood there holding the door even after Bella and Megan walked away. She was deeply controlled.

Megan was a good five or six inches taller than the tiny vamp, but Bella didn't appear to exert any effort pulling the larger woman out of the car. Bella was an old vampire, and the older they were, the stronger they were.

Megan tried to jerk her handcuffed arm out of Bella's grasp, but she didn't even budge the vamp. I gasped—quietly—but Bella's gaze snapped over to me. She scanned all around, but my shadows held, and she didn't see me. The sun was touching the water in the west now, and soon it would plummet over the edge. That would be great for my gargoyle friends, but it would be good for the vamps as well. Bella didn't enjoy the sun, but since she was old, she could walk in it just fine. Younger vamps didn't have that luxury.

I was pretty sure, unless Vic had called in favors, his Vendetta didn't have many old members left. We'd decimated them. That's why he was using the police, and no vampires were out here guarding their retreat.

That meant we'd probably be up to our eyeballs in new vampires once the sun went down. I looked around nervously. Still no one else but the cops and Bella. I watched Megan as Bella dragged her down to the dock entrance. Megan had blood smeared on her throat. Dammit, Bella had bitten her! I wanted to set the tiny vamp on fire, but I couldn't as long as she hung on to Megan. Luke stepped in front of them before they started down the pathway.

"Get out of my way!" Bella yelled.

Luke stiffened and started to back up, but then stopped. Bella was a force, and that command had been hard to resist.

"Let go of her," Luke growled.

Bella grinned. I shivered. "I don't think so, wolf. Now move, or I'll move you."

"You aren't going one more step with her. She's mine." Luke's eyes flashed gold. Megan stopped, and Bella dragged her for two steps.

"Silly wolf. She's almost mine. One more bite, a little of my blood, and well…" she laughed again.

I felt the blood leave my face.

That was enough for Luke. He leapt at Bella, his huge wolf ripping through the borrowed clothing. He hit her hard, and they both crumpled to the ground. I ran forward and grabbed Megan. Luke squealed.

I walked and dropped Megan off at the practice planet. "Stay right here," I commanded. Megan started to protest, but I ignored her and walked back. Gabe and the gargoyles were running up the ramp from the dock. Bella and Luke were circling each other, Luke's shoulder dripped blood. I knew werewolves healed fast, so I figured it would close up soon. Bella was snarling, her teeth increasing in length until they didn't look like they'd fit in her mouth. Then she unhinged her jaw, and her maw increased hideously. She threw herself on Luke, teeth gnashing. Luke spun, but she was on his back, and he couldn't get a hold of her.

I gathered up my fire magic to throw at her, but just then a Whelan construction truck slid to a stop five feet away, and Noah jumped out. He took two steps and shifted into his wolf. The huge black beast snapped his teeth on Bella and ripped her off Luke. Madison exited the truck and also shifted. Seeing all of us, Bella jumped into the air, shifted into her large, man-sized bat form, and flew off towards the yacht. In the confusion, with everything happening at once, I didn't have time to react, and Bella was too far away for my erratic lightning bolts.

With her gone, the police officers froze in confusion. Bella's hold was easing, and soon the officers looked around in a state of confusion. The werewolves faded into the background, staying out of sight. It would be hard to explain three gigantic wolves to the cops. Luckily, darkness fell, and the wolves could slip out the sight of the humans.

However, that wasn't as obvious as the gargoyle that leapt up the second the darkness fell. I didn't even get a chance to use my shadow magic to help them, but the gargoyle raced after Bella, and the others followed close behind. I had to deal with the humans first. I sighed.

"What happened?" Officer Lopez said.

"I think that small woman drugged you," I said.

"Who?"

I sighed. "Her name is Bella Tarquino. For some reason, she and her boss, Vic Constantine, are on a mission to put me out of business. You came and arrested my friend from my B&B tonight. Do you remember that?"

"Sort of. It's like a dream."

"She drugged you and used some kind of mind control. You'll want to get checked out."

"Yeah, thanks."

She must have been very disoriented, or the vamp mind control was still affecting her, because she believed everything I said, gathered up the other officers and they all left. I hoped they were safe to drive.

I turned my attention back to my friends. The wolves had changed back and dressed while I was talking to the police officer.

Another truck pulled up, and Jim and Chef Jack jumped out. They looked around confused.

"What's going on?" I asked Gabe, since the last thing I'd seen were the gargoyles chasing Bella.

"They haven't come back yet."

"Shit, they could be in trouble, and none of us can fly." I looked at Gabe, but he shrugged. He didn't have any ideas either.

"I can," Jim said. Yes, in his Quetzalcoatl form, he could fly.

"Could you take any passengers?"

"No."

I didn't know if one Quetzalcoatl could take down a yacht of vamps if the gargoyles were out of commission.

"We can grab a boat and head out to the yacht," Noah suggested. I looked around. It was past time for anyone to rent to us, it was dark, and I didn't own a boat.

"Did you mean take one, or do you have one?" I asked.

Noah smiled. "Let me make a call." He turned and jogged to his truck.

I guessed he knew someone with a boat. However, by the time we had permission, had the boat ready, and left, whatever was happening would probably be over. I sighed. I could always take us back in time, again.

"Where's Megan?" Luke asked looking around.

"She's safe. I took her to the practice planet."

"Is it safe there? She doesn't have a protector?"

I blanched. I didn't know. There could be predators there, and the Fae used it to practice realm walking.

"I don't know. Come on, I'll take you there."

Luke held out his hand. I looked at Gabe, asking with my eyes if he wanted to go. He nodded and grasped my other hand. We walked.

Chapter Five

Megan was where I'd left her, but she wasn't safe. The longest I'd stayed on the practice planet was maybe a couple of minutes. But Megan had been there for about twenty. And apparently it had predators. She was surrounded by a pack of wolves—in the loosest sense of the word. These were not earthly wolves and didn't resemble them at all, except in the intent they were directing at Megan. They were scaled, clawed, the size of Mr. Mittens in Splintercat form, and apparently hungry.

Megan had her spear and shield. The cops hadn't searched her, and Bella hadn't considered her a threat at all. The two marbles in her pockets were concentrated magic and formed into weapons when she used her magic words.

She rotated around, poking at one of the three creatures if it got to close. Luke ripped his hand free of my grip and leaped in to stand at her back. I looked for an entrance so I could just grab her and realm walk her away.

One of the creatures lunged forward at her. They hadn't noticed me and Gabe yet, so I used a puff of air magic to push it away. It stumbled into one of the other creatures, and once they righted themselves, they saw us. I thought one of them would rush us, but they gave this odd burping cry that ended in a high-pitched screech. There was an answering call in the distance.

"It's time to go guys!" I yelled, and they agreed. Luke yanked Megan back from one creature still aggressively lunging, and I took the opportunity to blast all three creatures back with my air magic. They tumbled around, disoriented and far enough away that Gabe and I could run in. We grabbed hands and walked back to the dock on earth. I figured it was safe for Megan there now.

We'd been gone less than a minute, but Noah called out the minute we materialized, "We have an idea!"

It took me a minute to figure out what he was saying, but we all gathered round.

"We don't have a boat with a motor, but there is a rowboat tied up. Jim can pull us into the boat, and we can go now. If they leave at slack tide, we'll lose our chance."

I looked at Jim. He was as calm and composed as ever. "You're willing?" I asked. I couldn't ask anyone to fight my battles or break laws in my name. It had to be their own free will.

"Yes."

"OK, who's going? How many will fit in the boat?"

"Six," Noah said. "Jim will be flying, so Jack, me, Luke, you, Gabe, and Madison."

"I'm going," Megan said. It was the first time I'd heard her speak since this all happened. She cleared her throat and clutched it as though it were sore. It must be the new vampire bite.

Gabe leaned over and touched his hand to her shoulder, healing her. She gave a sigh of relief. "Thanks."

"You should stay here, and someone will stay with you," Luke said.

"This is my fight," Megan argued, her jaw set in her stubborn expression. Her last vamp experience had messed her up emotionally, and she was fighting the effects by literally plunging herself into weapons and learning to fight. She started learning before the vamps, but they'd driven her to obsession. Her weapons made her feel safe.

"The vampires are after you," he said. "We'd be delivering you to their hands."

"I'm not going alone."

Luke threw up his hands. I understood. I'd been dealing with her stubborn streak for years. And now that her PTSD was part of the equation, that streak had gotten worse. I wanted her to stay, but at the same time it was her fight, and part of her healing.

"We need to go. We're losing time," Gabe reminded everyone.

Madison stayed back so Megan could go. Since working together so much, she and Megan were growing closer, so I figured she was on Megan's side, anyway. We clambered into the boat, and Jim, standing on the dock, grasped the mooring line in his teeth. Then he shimmered, and his feathered serpent form appeared, floating in the air, wingless. I still found the sight amazing. He tugged gently, and soon we were racing over the luckily smooth waters of Tillamook Bay.

The yacht was moving slowly. It had started to turn toward the bar where the exit to the bay was. Jim sped up. We were traveling much faster than a motor could move us. Still no sign of the gargoyles. They must be in deep trouble. It didn't take us long to get there. No one was on the outer decks of the yacht. Jim landed on the lower deck of the stern and shifted back to his human shape. He tied off the boat, and we climbed on board as silently as possible. Noah, Luke, and Chef Jack shifted into their animal forms. They were faster and stronger that way. Megan reactivated her weapons, and Jim once more shimmered into his feathered serpent form.

The yacht had two deck levels, and a level below the water. It stood tall, as big or bigger than many of the fishing boats around. We spread out. Gabe opened the lower hatches to access that level for the men in animal form, and Megan and I headed in on the first deck where we'd disembarked.

The yacht, although it was moving towards the bay exit, was silent as death. I shivered at that thought. Where was the engine noise? The people? Where were Sam and the other two gargoyles?

Something was off. I seemed to remember that vampires weren't supposed to be able to cross running water. Or was that witches? Was ocean water running water? Those were questions I didn't need my brain to focus on right now. I shoved them away. I needed to focus.

Megan and I entered through a sliding glass door on the first deck level at the stern. The perfect opulence of the yacht was evident. It had thick rich carpet, glistening, high polished wood, and luxurious couches. Still, not one other person. We continued past the built in wet bar, and down a short corridor lined with three doors. We opened rooms as we went. Guest rooms, I assumed since they contained beds. Where was everyone?

We made our way up the stairs to the second deck level and helm. Someone had to be at the helm; the boat was moving. Megan was close behind me. I threw open the door and froze at the sight before me.

"It's a trap," I screamed, and threw myself back into Megan and down the stairs as the boat exploded. I instinctively cushioned us with air, and as we were hurtled down the stairs we'd just walked up, I used the movement to walk us to the practice planet, and then back to the dock.

Nothing was left, but some smoke and wreckage on the water. My heart stopped, and my stomach fell. Megan and I were scorched and beat up.

I felt numb. I walked us to the house. As we stepped into the back parking lot, it hit me. Everyone was gone. I gasped and grabbed my stomach to stop the pain. The sobs bubbled up uncontrollably. I had to go back and try to find a way to stop us from getting on the yacht. I needed to calm down and think. Otherwise, they were all dead. Gabe... I sobbed harder, gasping.

Megan gripped my shoulders. I couldn't look at her. She shook me. I couldn't breathe.

"Sorry, Brigid." I heard her murmur before she slapped me. That startled me long enough to breathe and look at her. She grabbed my hand and pulled me into the kitchen. She pushed me into a chair and put her hands on my shoulders so she could look into my eyes.

"You can still save them. Pull yourself together," she hissed. Her eyes were also red, and her face flushed with emotion. "Luke was there too."

I nodded. Right. I needed to do this. I stood, and went to walk forward, to realm walk, but Megan grabbed me. "Do you have your phone?"

I checked my pockets. Yes, it was in my back pocket. I nodded.

"Do you know where and when you are going?"

I didn't. I wasn't thinking straight. Without a destination,

I could get lost. I needed to be clear-headed. I also needed to renew my magic close to the Faerie link. That meant a trip to the waterfall. No one was dead. Not yet. I'd save them. I had to keep that firmly in my mind to keep from losing it again.

"Mr. Mittens!" I sent out a loud mental call to my cat. I needed him to keep me focused. I had to save them, and I had to keep my head on straight.

"You'll do it. I know you will," Megan said.

My breath shuddered, and I wiped my eyes. I nodded. I could do this.

Mr. Mittens appeared from the house side and came right at us.

He looked into my face.

What happened?

Sometimes my cat was better at reading me than a human could.

I shook my head and held back the sobs. "I can still save them; I just need to go to the waterfall." It was all I could get out.

Let's go, he said.

We followed him out the door, across the parking lot, and up the twisting trail to the waterfall a mile away. The power started filling my cells and recharging me as we went. On the property, it wasn't a problem to stay recharged, but I'd realm walked a lot away from home, and the result was draining. I couldn't imagine being full Fae and used to the ambient magic there and then coming here. It was a marked difference. I knew now, after my visit to Faerie, why my great-grandfather couldn't or didn't want to stay on earth for long periods of time.

I couldn't do anything but wait while the power seeping here from Faerie filled my reserves.

I do hate to bother you now, but we also had some excitement here, Mr. Mittens said.

I looked at him. "Not more vampires?" It would be just like the slimy creatures to come back here after they laid their trap.

No. Griffins. Two large griffins came looking for Brightfeather.

Dread filled my heart as I remembered the promise I'd made to my griffin friend.

"What did they want?"

I don't know. When I told them I didn't know where she was, they left.

"Are you sure they're gone, or are they searching the property?"

They are gone. I'd sense them if they remained here, he said with a sniff.

"I wasn't insulting you. Brightfeather has a secret she wants to keep from her husband's family. If they've already come looking for her, we're running out of time."

He cocked his head at me. *Hmpf. I would not lead Bright-feather into danger.*

"I know, my friend." I stood up from the rock I'd been sitting on. "We can go, I've got enough."

Before he could answer, a bright flash interrupted us. I covered up my eyes and blinked the spots away.

Chapter Six

"Granddaughter," a familiar booming voice declared. I gazed up at my Fae great-grandfather.

I almost sobbed in relief. The cavalry was here. I could do this now.

He took one look at my face and Megan's and frowned. "What tragedy has befallen?"

His presence triggered the emotions I'd been holding back, and I couldn't speak. His gaze swung to Mr. Mittens, who filled him in.

"You seek to traverse time?" he questioned.

I nodded. He was familiar with that human response.

He took a deep breath. "I will help you."

A weight lifted from my shoulders. I just needed to stop us from going to the boat. No, I needed to stop the gargoyles from pursuing Bella. It had been a setup from the beginning. Sure, they'd taken Megan, but we got her back easily, really. They'd been trying to take us out in one blow, and they nearly succeeded. We'd eagerly jumped into their trap. They were probably long gone somewhere, laughing over their blood meals and dancing on my grave. I *hated* vampires.

The only person remaining back at the harbor was Madison. She must be beside herself. She'd just seen us all go up in a fireball. Well, it wouldn't matter soon. We'd go back and stop it all. I pictured the perfect time. Bella had just flown off, and the gargoyles hadn't quite shifted yet. I grabbed Megan's and my grandfather's hands and walked.

We walked to the practice planet. The creatures we'd battled were gone, their prey out of reach. I only took an instant to scan for them, and then we were back at the dock. I'd put us down at the ramp near the gargoyles, since they were getting ready to chase Bella, who was flying over us towards the rigged yacht. Sam shifted first. We'd arrived in time.

"Stop!" I commanded him, and his gruesome face turned towards me.

"It's a trap. We've come back from the future to warn you not to go to the boat. It's rigged to blow, and we walked directly into the trap. We have to let the vamps go for now."

Sam froze and shifted back. Together, we walked up the ramp to stop the rest of the group from going to the yacht. Although the gargoyles hadn't followed Bella, it wasn't likely we would either. I hung back. I didn't know what would happen if Megan and I faced ourselves in the same time. It already felt like feedback in my ears, and my guts ached. I stopped and let my grandfather and the gargoyles move ahead.

"Do you feel that?" I asked Megan.

She frowned. "No, feel what?"

That's right, I hadn't rescued her from the practice planet yet. She didn't feel what I did.

We stopped. I couldn't go further. It was like trying to

squeeze two magnets together when they wanted to repel each other. I could hear my voice up ahead say, "What is that?"

We had to go back to our time and let everything work itself out. That was the logical thing to do. "We have to go back to our time," I said. Megan shrugged. I grabbed her hand again, and we walked.

I looked up to see my grandfather and the gargoyles walking up the ramp towards us. I gasped. "Grandfather?" I said, shocked. "What are you doing here?"

He laughed. "You brought me here, but I felt you leave again. It's hard to occupy the same space at the same time. I assume you and your friend walked, and the timelines merged."

I shook my head. I had no memory of it. But I was here, and I guess this was the past to grandfather. Bella had left, and now all I had to do was fetch Megan and go home. We'd be better prepared if they tried again.

Then a feeling of despair washed over me. Something bad had happened or I wouldn't have brought my grandfather here. "What happened?"

He frowned. "You told me the vampires set a trap for you on a boat, and you all fell for it and were killed. My message is don't get on any boats."

I looked around at Gabe and my friends, and my heart tightened. I couldn't bear to lose one of them. "Let's go home," I said. "Who knows what they'll do next if we don't spring the trap. We'll have to watch our backs."

As groups climbed into the two vehicles, Gabe, my grandfather, and I grasped hands to walk back to the practice planet. Before we stepped, an immense explosion pounded against us with physical force. A glance at the bay showed a fireball where the yacht had been. My heart clenched, and I was happy that future me had saved my friends. We walked.

Megan was standing in a field surrounded by three strange beasts. They were scaled, clawed, and the size of Mr. Mittens in his Splintercat form. I readied my lightning to blast the one furthest back. Grandfather raised a hand to stop me. He pulled on a silver chain around his neck, tugging it from his shirt. There was a pendant of some sort hanging from it. He lifted it to his lips and blew on it. The creatures whined and ran off.

That wasn't what I'd been expecting, but Megan was relieved. Her spear dropped, and then her weapons retracted back into the magic balls, and she dropped them into her pocket. "What took you so long?" she asked. "I was about to become wolflizard dinner."

"Wolflizard?" I asked with a laugh.

"You have a better word for scaly critters that want to eat me?"

"Nope, wolflizard is perfect. Let's go home."

"I'm ready, believe me."

She added her hand to the mix, and we walked home.

Once there, while we waited for the others that had taken vehicles, I asked my grandfather, "What was that pendant thing?"

He pulled it out of his shirt again. "It is simply a whistle with an irritating frequency. Works wonders against scalawargs."

"I gather that's the name of the wolflizards?"

"Yes."

"Grandfather, I'm very grateful you came, even if there wasn't anything for you to do. I must have been at a loss."

"It is a small matter to come when I am needed. Besides, court has calmed down some, and a new Phoenix has been chosen."

"Really? That's awesome!" He was filling in after the last Phoenix had been discovered plotting against the king of the Fae. However, my grandfather hated politics and was itching for the position to be filled so he could go back to doing what he enjoyed most. War. He was still the king's Pendragon.

"I am rightfully relieved," he remarked.

I smiled warmly at him. "Can I get you something to drink?"

"If you are safe and have no more need of me, I shall retire to my home. I haven't spent much time there lately."

"I think we're good."

"If things become worse, please summon me."

"I will." I almost thanked him but stopped myself. He stepped outside the door, and a flash of light let us know he'd walked back home.

Chapter Seven

I was worried about Megan. She'd seemed fine, after being attacked and kidnapped by the vamps, and being used as a juice box, but I knew she wasn't. She kept saying, "I'm fine," but the haunted look was back in her eyes, and I caught her fingering the magic weapon balls in her pocket where she didn't think I'd notice.

She'd had such a rough time after Vic Constantine had attacked her. Working with Dana on the sly and building her weapon and fighting skills had helped. But I didn't know how to help her psychologically other than to suggest she see someone. She'd brushed me off more than once with her "I'm fine" comments to the point I just watched for the day and hoped that I would catch her before she snapped.

Now that we were headed home, I felt all the stress and worry leave me. I wanted to go to bed, but we had a new load of guests arriving tomorrow afternoon, and the things I wanted to get done after dinner had been delayed.

I did spend a few glorious moments telling Gabe good-night at his car. I came in flushed, with swollen lips and a goofy grin—which always made a night lovely. I went in determined to finish up quickly.

Our number one new rule was no vampires in the inn. We already had one about witches. Luckily, we hadn't had to turn anyone away yet, since our first vampire client had bailed early after driving us crazy with his picky demands.

Megan had come up with a better questionnaire from the first week the inn had been open, and now we knew what our clients were and what dietary needs they had. I knew Chef Jack appreciated that. When he wasn't helping us fight vampires in his tiger form, he was a brilliant cook who could make anything from chicken nuggets to Beef Wellington on demand.

I did my final check of the rooms. Since we'd had a rare day with no guests, everything was clean and ready to go. I'd been lucky and hadn't lost any cleaning staff after a poltergeist had been set loose in my inn. I had lost an employee at the creature stables because of the vampire war, though. Jim had hired a replacement. A young werewolf from the Whelan pack—they had a few members not in the family.

Once Chef Jack was back, I double checked the menus and supplies and fed Mr. Mittens his premium supper. It looked like we were ready. Now, I could relax in my tub. I was hoping we wouldn't have any run-ins with the vamps for a while. We'd ruined their trap, and I knew their numbers were decimated. I hoped the master and his creepy enforcer had fled to Europe or wherever they'd come from. I mean, I'd won fair and square.

Our incoming guests for the inn proper were a husband-and-wife shifter couple, a psychic, a small family of kitsune, and a mixed-race couple. He was an angel. That was unique for me. I didn't know that angels were even allowed to marry. I was extremely curious. On top of that, his wife was human. Since she already knew about supernaturals, it wasn't a problem. My first human guest had been a horror. She'd brought her pet poltergeist and set it loose to wreak havoc and destroy my inn. One of the reasons we now had a questionnaire.

I knew next to nothing about this particular group of supernaturals, because other than a few shifters, particularly werewolves, one tiger, and Quetzalcoatl, I didn't know much about any of the supernatural types coming to stay. Jim had a better handle on his guests, since they were creatures he was familiar with. We had a wyvern coming, a full kelpie from Faerie, which made me a little nervous, and a minotaur.

I shut my bathroom door with a relieved sigh. I'd earned this bath today, and I wanted a soak. I was staying in the water until it turned cold. I might even refill it with hot water and stay double time.

I filled my glorious soaking tub and dumped the perfumed salts into it. I was at the age where bubbles were fine, but Epsom salts were a must. As the tub filled, I stripped and then lowered myself in gratefully.

Part of me waited for yelling to begin, vampires to attack, or something else to ruin my night, but I was allowed my soak for once.

I'd just climbed out and wrapped myself in a towel when Megan burst into my bathroom. I was startled enough I almost dropped my towel.

"Brigid!"

"Is something on fire? Are the vampires back?" I asked while the worst-case scenarios ran through my brain.

"No. It's worse. It's Goch."

Immediately, my mind went to sickness or injury with my teenage dragon. "What's wrong?"

"You just need to see."

I threw on my robe and slipped on some flip-flops. With my hair up in a towel, I followed Megan out the back kitchen door onto the large porch.

Goch was in the parking lot, luckily the cars that were parked there were off to the side, including my new SUV. The old one had been squished by said dragon in an exuberant landing after he realm walked alone the first time. His head was down and facing away from the house. We had a clear view of his tail and backside, though.

"So, what's wrong?" I whispered to Megan.

"Just wait," she said. "Goch, I brought Brigid."

His sides heaved in and out in a dragon sized sigh. Then he swung his head to look at me. I gasped. He had two horns growing on his head, a new development, but now one of them was snapped off, and his face had a distinct claw mark down the right side.

I ran out to him. "What happened?"

He continued to look down as though ashamed.

"Goch, you have to tell me."

He looked over at Megan, and she also pressed him to answer.

I did something stupid.

Clearly. But I held my tongue. He already felt embarrassed enough and hurt. The claw mark on his face looked painful.

"Are you badly hurt?" I asked before I pushed harder for an explanation.

Just my face, and my poor horn! he wailed. *No mate will want me now!*

"Why not?" I asked. A broken horn and scars hardly seemed like it would keep a potential mate away.

I'm scarred and hideous! Dragon snot dripped from his nose. I couldn't deal with an angsted-out teen dragon.

"Goch, take a deep breath. Girls like scars. It'll be fine."

They do?

I thought of the stupid things I'd done in college, and I went through a small bad boy phase, so I did know what I was talking about.

"Yes, you look tough and capable. Females eat that stuff up. Now, calm down and tell me what happened."

He breathed in and out until his breath was steady again, and his nose stopped dripping.

Mr. Mittens took me hunting on his home planet. He warned me not to hunt the Xlstlsdf. But they were so small. So much smaller than me. I knew I could kill it with my wings tied down. He shook his head, and it sunk down even further. *But Mr. Mittens was right. He had to save me.*

I looked around for my cat. Did this happen after he ate his supper? Was he hurt as well?

"Is Mr. Mittens back?" I asked, trying to keep my voice calm. The dragon was already upset enough.

Yes, he went to the waterfall. He said he needed to be away from my stupidity. He started wailing again.

Sometimes my cat could be an asshole.

"I'm sure he'll get over it soon. He has a hot head," I said to reassure him. Mr. Mittens must have been hurt. He didn't have a very hot head, and it took a lot to annoy him to that level. Mostly, he just showed disdain.

He'll never want to take me hunting again!

That was his real worry, I could tell. "Nonsense. You'll be hunting again soon. You can't worry about it. Now, let's take care of those nasty scratches before they get infected." I looked over at Megan. She already had a bottle of alcohol and a large tube of triple antibiotic cream. I wondered if I should use one of Dana's magic healing balls, but even though she'd replaced the ones I used a few months ago, they were best to save for dire need.

"Goch, lower your head. I'm going to treat your wounds." He lowered his head and laid it on the ground in front of me. "This is going to sting. Just make sure you don't move, or you'll send me flying, OK?"

Yes, Brigid. I'll be careful.

I took the large bottle and started pouring it on the claw marks. I heard Goch's sucked in breath when the disinfectant hit the wounds, but he held still. Once they were washed clean, and hopefully free of whatever bacteria came from the creature's claws, I slathered the whole tube of cream on the scratches. One was really close to his eye. I also examined his horn.

"Does your horn hurt?" I asked him.

It aches, but not as bad as my face.

"Will it grow back?"

I don't think so. At least the dragons I knew with broken horns didn't have them grow back, he said.

"Well, there's no sense worrying about it. I don't know if I should pack it with something so it won't ache, but it probably just needs time."

I didn't have an aspirin or Tylenol big enough for a dragon, either. I should probably see if Dana could make some pain reliever for the larger members of my little kingdom. Gabe had to work four ten-hour shifts the next four days, or I'd call him. He wasn't as comfortable with the creatures as he was with the people, though.

Once I was done, I reassured him again, and told him to

find his nest and rest. He thanked me and launched himself into the air.

Once he was gone, I turned to Megan. "Maybe I should have encouraged him to go back to his mom."

She shrugged. "We were teenagers once. We did stupid stuff, too. It's all part of growing up."

"Yeah, but he's not my kid. If he came back hurt badly, or if he was killed, how would I explain that to the dragons? To his mom?"

"She left him here. Not your bad."

I nodded, but I still felt slightly sick that he'd been permanently disfigured on my watch.

Chapter Eight

My stress level between the vamps, Megan, and Goch was high, but regardless, I slept well. Which was a relief. Our first arrival was the angel and his human wife. I was dying to see what an angel looked like, so I was deeply disappointed when he just looked like a regular guy. He was handsome, well-built, and a distance over six feet because I had to look up at him. He had light brown hair and light gold eyes. She was also normal looking. You'd think that an angel would have only been snagged by someone of extreme beauty, or something. She had lovely, long, platinum blonde hair that looked natural and dark brown eyes. But other than her hair, you wouldn't look at her twice.

I greeted them, and after Megan checked them in, I gave them a short tour of the dining room and elevator and explained how to get to their room. Thirty minutes later, the kitsune family arrived. They were of Asian descent, I assumed Japanese, but were coming from Kentucky. The husband and wife were both handsome, and their three children were adorable. I put them in the largest room—the turret room on the third floor. I'd saved that for families since it had an extra room with a pull-out bed. One of the children was a toddler, so I asked if they wanted a crib. They did. I kept one in the attic, so after they were checked in and headed up, I followed to get the crib.

Mr. Mittens met me at the attic door. *I don't like them.*

"Who?" I asked, distracted.

Those you just placed. They smell funny.

I laughed. "It's because they are fox shifters."

His lip curled. *Hmpf.*

He wandered down the corridor, pausing at their door and giving a loud sniff. Then he hurried down the stairs.

I watched him, shaking my head. I retrieved the crib, rolling it down the hall to the kitsune's door. I gave two sharp knocks. The mom opened the door and thanked me. She rolled it in.

The psychic came next. I guess I was expecting someone like Luke and Madison's Aunt Zella, who liked to dress in colorful muumuus and wore crazy hats. But she just looked normal. Maybe mid-thirties, reddish brown hair pulled back in a ponytail and wearing jeans and a long-sleeved t-shirt. I was a little disappointed. Looking at Megan, she was too.

Last of the bunch was the shifter couple. They hadn't listed what they shifted into, and I hoped that didn't come back to bite us. They looked to be around mine and Megan's age, probably escaping jobs and family responsibilities for a vacation.

Once they were checked in, Megan and I high fived. A good check-in with no problems was always a relief.

"How are you feeling?" I asked her once everyone was securely in their rooms.

She shrugged. "Fine, maybe a little tired, but Bella only drank a small amount."

"And you remember everything?"

She shuddered. "Yeah. Wish I didn't."

"Did they say anything or give anything away?"

She shrugged.

I assumed that meant nothing important was said around her. I also sensed she didn't want to talk about it, so I told her about Mr. Mittens and the kitsune family.

She laughed. "Too bad he can't smell crazy like Jessica and her poltergeist."

"I know, right?"

The rest of the day was uneventful. I even went to bed without feeling stressed. It didn't last.

Madison had the first shift in the morning. I wandered into the dining room to pick up some breakfast. Chef Jack had made crepes today, and my mouth watered as I loaded mine up. I went into the kitchen to eat and feed Mr. Mittens. Megan was already there, tucking into her second crepe.

"These are to die for," she said to Jack as I swung in through the door.

He chuckled. "Thanks."

Megan looked up at me. "We've already had a complaint this morning."

I looked at her sharply. "About what?"

"The kitsune family being too loud. Particularly, the children running and jumping.

"Their room is directly over yours. Did you hear them?"

"Yeah, a little, but I think it was the running in the hallway at six this morning that did it."

I sighed. Here we go again. "Who was the complainer?"

"The couple on three, and the psychic on two."

"So, everyone but the shifters?"

"Yup, but only because they left early."

"I'll go speak to them."

"Already did."

"Oh, thanks!"

"They told me to mind my business."

"They what?" I could feel my cheeks flush with anger.

"It was done politely, and they did apologize, sort of."

"What did they say, exactly?" I could see that I was missing some information.

She looked up and to the left, thinking. "Umm, sorry that the children are loud, they have a hard time staying contained in a such a small room, but we have it handled. Or something like that."

"Such a small room?" My temper was definitely flaring. I took a few deep breaths. "That is the biggest room in the house!"

She shrugged. She knew. Rude guests were so fun. Oh well, I could put up with anything for a week. I took another slow steady breath.

"At least they left for the day."

"Thank heavens."

"The angel couple and the psychic are in the dining room."

"Yeah, I saw them."

"Any news on the stables? Did our creature guests arrive?"

"Oh, yeah, Jim came by. Said all was well."

"Well, that's good news. I've been a little worried about the kelpie."

"As long as he doesn't lure anyone into any water, we should be fine."

That was a possible problem. After our problem with

the vampires, and the first week of guests, I'd been concerned we'd never have another guest—mainly because my first two guests had been murdered, one had been forced out by the vampires, a couple had been chased away by the poltergeist thing, and the woman that had loosed the ghost had tried to destroy me on social media. So, I had Jim put in a small fishing pond we stocked with trout as a draw.

It was an add-on in price if a guest wanted to take out a canoe and fish, or fish from the tiny dock, but it had been popular so far. The only reason I had accepted the kelpie this week is that no one in this batch had requested the fishing pond, so I hoped it wouldn't be a problem. Located by the old dairy, the pond was out of the way of the main house.

"Yeah, I'm sure the kelpie is on his best behavior. I'm just being weird," I said.

Megan gave a positive sounding grunt since her mouth was full.

"Everything will be perfect, right?" I asked.

She gave me a thumbs up.

Just then, the maids arrived. I wasn't a big chain, so I didn't hire directly. I worked with a cleaning company. They were human, but knew about supernaturals, because they'd cleaned the offices at the fish plant where the witches, and now vampires, worked their evil. I only took them because they weren't witches and had been victimized by them as well.

They'd gratefully taken me on, and even a naughty poltergeist hadn't scared them away. I made sure to pay on time and leave healthy tips for the two maids that kept me in business. Lupita and Agnes seemed to take crazy in style.

I waved to them as they put away their jackets and bags in the makeshift lockers in the laundry room. One of the few perks I offered were free meals, so they liked to start early and grab breakfast. Megan and I were done, so we cleared our dishes and left the kitchen to the two women.

I headed up front to check on Madison when I received a desperate mental message.

Brigid, come quick! My eggs are hatching! Brightfeather's mental voice was a mix of terror and joy.

I turned to Megan with a big smile.

"Wanna go see baby griffins?"

"Are unicorns huge dicks?"

"We've been summoned!"

I didn't know how to find Brightfeather's nest by walking through my woods. I know my cat expected me to be able to locate a single blade of grass on the other side, but I hadn't mastered that yet. However, I did remember it well enough to walk to it.

"I have to realm walk us. I don't know the way."

She shrugged and held out her hand. I grasped it and walked us to the practice planet, and then with another step we were at Brightfeather's nest.

Chapter Nine

The nest was more like a globe with a protected opening to block any weather. It was large as well, since a griffin in its true form was roughly the size of a draft horse with enormous wings.

Once we materialized, I called out to Brightfeather. You did not want to surprise a new griffin mother.

Come inside, Brigid and Megan, she said.

We entered.

Brightfeather was crouched over her three eggs. Her wings were partially unfurled, and she was watching them intently. The eggs wobbled, but no cracks had yet appeared.

"What's the protocol?" Megan whispered to me.

I shrugged; this was my first griffin birth as well. "Brightfeather, what do we need to do to help you?"

Just stay with me. All else is prepared. She glanced briefly to her right, and I noticed three large, skinned rabbits waiting.

So we sat, legs crossed, and waited. About fifteen minutes after we arrived, the eggs rocked violently, and one finally cracked with a loud snapping sound. I moved to my knees to see better. Brightfeather's eyes glistened with excitement. My heart warmed for her.

The second egg snapped. It was happening faster now. The first egg had a small beak poking through, and I wondered for a moment if we'd get an eagle griffin, or an owl like their father, or something completely different. I had no idea how griffin genetics worked.

The third egg was still wobbling. It hadn't cracked yet, and I was growing worried. I looked at Brightfeather, but she didn't seem concerned.

A little head finally burst from the first egg, and Brightfeather carefully removed the part of the shell that clung to its little skull. A tiny eagle head cheeped at us. I smiled. It wobbled clear of its shell and stumbled a little. Brightfeather tore off a hunk of meat from a rabbit and stuffed it into the little open beak. It fell over, and Megan and I giggled at the cuteness. The third egg gave a violent wobble and went still. But Brightfeather was busy shoving rabbit into two hungry beaks now.

"It's not moving," I said to her.

She glanced at the third egg. "Not all eggs hatch." I could sense her sadness, but I couldn't let the little one die.

"Shouldn't we crack open the shell?" I asked.

"That is not our way. If it cannot break free, it will not survive."

"Well, it should have a chance, anyway."

Brightfeather hesitated, her head cocked to the side. Then she nodded. "Yes. It is time to change the old ways." She fed another piece of meat to her second baby, and then tapped the unbroken shell with her mighty beak. It cracked. Megan and I pulled the shell free of the tiny griffin. I gasped. It wasn't an eagle like the other two. It was an owlet, and its beak wasn't as large or heavy as the two eaglets. That's why it struggled.

It attempted to get its four feet under it. It took a step and fell right into my lap. I gathered up the damp creature, and its bright golden eyes met mine. It gave me a sharp *cheep*. I laughed, and Brightfeather flipped a rabbit carcass to me. Megan and I tore meat from it and fed the little one until its tiny belly was hard and full. Then I tucked it in with its siblings to sleep. Being born was tiring work.

"They're perfect, Brightfeather," I whispered.

She practically glowed with happiness. *Thank you for being here. I was...frightened to be alone.*

"You are welcome. Have you thought of names?" I didn't even know if they were boys or girls.

Yes, although it will be another break from tradition. Usually, they aren't named until they are presented to griffin society at large, but I cannot do that. So, for my firstborn, I believe I will name him for his father, Umber. The second, I will name for my father, Brightstorm, and my precious little girl, who might not have been born if I didn't have friends, I'd like to name after you, Brigid.

My throat closed with tears. I swallowed hard. "I'd be honored."

Brightfeather bowed her head at me. *It is so.*

Megan and I left the little family to rest. I walked us back to the house.

When we materialized on the back porch, Mr. Mittens was waiting.

Did you wander the property without me? he demanded.

"No, your bossiness. We were summoned by Brightfeather. Her eggs hatched! She has three perfect griffinettes," Megan announced.

I kept my grin behind my hand so my cat wouldn't be mad at me.

Hmpf. He flipped his tail, annoyed that he hadn't been there to protect me from my own woods.

"She is so happy," I added.

He turned his blazing blue gaze on me.

"I'm sure if you stop in with some meat, she'll let you see them," I offered as a white flag. I think he was a little hurt he hadn't been invited to the birth. He didn't realize it was a female thing. She'd wanted help and support.

Is that a common offering for those newly born? he asked, and I sensed his curiosity.

"I'm sure it is for griffin babies."

He considered it. Then he jumped down off the porch railing and wandered off.

Before I opened the door into the kitchen, I felt the drumming of huge wings. I stepped out from under the porch as Goch back winged above the parking lot. I checked that all vehicles were safe and waited for him.

"How are you feeling today?" I asked.

He brought his enormous head down for me to examine. He turned it so Megan could look at his horn while I examined the claw marks. They looked fine, no sign of infection. It wasn't hot to the touch or puffy.

I am fine. The ache in my horn is gone, although it hurts if I catch it on the trees. My face is not as painful as last night.

"Well, it looks good."

Do you think Mr. Mittens will talk to me today? he asked sadly.

Megan frowned at me.

"I don't know, sweetie. I think you need to give him another day, then just ask him."

His head hung down again, and he dragged a clawed toe along the asphalt of the parking lot. It left a groove.

I stiffened, but let it go. Anything could be repaired.

"Why don't you choose a cow from the stock for now, and I'm sure you'll be back to realm hunting soon."

I mainly kept the stock for guests, but I could spare a cow now and then for emergencies.

That cheered him a little. *Thank you, Brigid!* And with that, he sprang into the air and beat his powerful wings.

"Ugh, I need to remember to wear a ponytail when we talk to Goch." Megan said, attempting to tame her hair in the windstorm created by Goch's wings. Since I was busy doing the same, I agreed.

It had been a good day. Worrying about the vamps and what they were planning next kept me from being truly happy, but otherwise, things were good.

Chapter Ten

"You have a dragon," a small, sweet voice said behind me. I whirled around. One of the kitsune children stood behind me on the porch. She was tiny, probably only four or five years old, but small for her age.

"He's not a pet, sweetie. He's his own person." I didn't want her to think I would let her pet Goch or treat him like a non-sentient creature.

"I want a dragon."

I probably did too at one time, before I knew how much work was involved. There was the whole sentient thing as well.

"Where's your mommy?" I asked. It wasn't my place to teach the child about, well, anything.

She jutted out her bottom lip. "I want a dragon!" This time she screamed it, stomped her foot, and started to wail.

I looked around. Megan had slipped inside before me and had escaped. I didn't have any experience with children, and now I knew why. I froze in my tracks. The little girl threw herself down on the wooden planks and kicked, screamed, pounded her tiny fists, and cried. I was torn. Did I leave her to go inside and try to find her mother, or pick her up and try to comfort her? Which would get me sued? I went inside.

Megan was standing by the door, laughing. "I saw the whole thing."

"You could have saved me."

"Nah, where's the fun in that?"

I glared at her. "Where's the mom?"

"Dining room."

"Ugh!"

I walked into the dining room. I'd thought the kitsunes had left for the day, but apparently, they were back for second breakfast. The mom and dad were eating alone. That confused me. They had a child small enough to require a crib. Why wasn't the toddler with them?

It wasn't my business. Maybe they were back because the baby had fallen asleep, and they put it down for a nap.

"Excuse me. Your daughter is distraught. She's out on the back porch."

They gave me a blank stare. Maybe they hadn't heard me, so I repeated myself.

The dad continued to eat. Mom only shrugged. "She'll get over it."

"Aren't you worried that she is outside alone?"

"I thought you said she was on the porch?"

"I did." However, I didn't know why that was relevant.

"She's fine." And mom dismissed me by going back to her food. I was shocked. But I couldn't make her more attentive. I left.

"How did it go?" Megan asked.

"She blew me off."

"It's her kid," Megan said, incredulously.

I shrugged. There wasn't anything else for me to do. Was I supposed to go out and watch the child? No. I couldn't cross that line. This was an inn, not a daycare.

Plus, as long as she stayed near the inn, she was perfectly safe. The trail to the waterfall was cloaked, and the pond with the kelpie was a distance from here. I had cameras outside and in the common areas because I'd been fighting evil witches and vampires, so I pulled the app up on my phone to keep a general eye on the kid and went about my business.

Megan must have done the same thing, because while I was in my drawing room office, working on the books, she came in.

"Those kids are all over the place."

I looked up, having forgotten about them, and pulled up the video feed again. Sure enough, the toddler was roaming the third floor. The boy, who looked slightly older than the girl from earlier, was sliding down the banister, and the girl was now outside on the front porch, lighting a box of matches. "Good hell in a handbasket," I said. "This is not a huge playpen."

"Do you want to take the little match girl or the parents?" Megan asked, her hand on her hip.

"I've already been ignored by the parents. You take a whirl." I stood up with a groan. I'd sat too long, and my back was stiff. I stretched and went out the front door to the girl who thought it was OK to light matches on the porch of a wooden house.

She had her back to me and was still striking matches, letting them burn, then dropping them. I walked up behind her and plucked the box from her hand.

"Hey!" she yelled. "Those are mine. Give them back."

"No."

I walked around her and stomped on the smoldering pile of matches until all the smoke stopped. Then I gathered my water magic and dumped it on the small pile. Once everything was completely out and cold to the touch, I swept the pile of ash off the porch with a puff of air magic.

She watched, fascinated by the magic. However, she was still mad that I'd taken the matches. "I'm telling my mom."

I was feeling equally juvenile, so I told her. "I'm telling her first." Then I stomped into the house, threw the matchbox into my fireplace, and set it on fire. Since it was magical flame, it lasted maybe fifteen seconds before it was all ash.

I couldn't imagine where the child had found a box of matches. All the fireplaces in the house had been converted to gas, and they didn't require lighting by match. Maybe we'd left a box by the barbecue grill out back, but I doubted it. So, she either snooped through the kitchen, where Chef Jack had lighters and matches for culinary purposes, or her parents had given her a box of matches. I couldn't imagine Chef Jack allowing a child in the kitchen, so I was left with the parents.

I walked back inside as Megan stormed down the stairs.

"What did the parents say?" I asked.

"How would I know? They wouldn't open their door or speak to me."

"Seriously?"

"Yes. Freaking unbelievable."

What was unbelievable was they'd stayed here all day, letting the children run around unsupervised. Didn't they worry they'd get hurt or burn down the building?

I grabbed my master key and headed back up the stairs.

Megan followed. I knocked politely on the door. When there was no answer, I knocked louder and said, "House-keeping." When that didn't get a response, I tapped my master key against the lock and opened the door. It only opened about four inches. They'd engaged the sliding lock. "Excuse me, Mr. and Mrs. Nishiyama," I yelled quite loudly. "You need to come and get your children. They cannot run around unsupervised."

Nothing. No response, no sounds of concern. I considered using my magic to open the door, but then an errant moan came drifting through the door, and I backed up and shut it. I looked at Megan. "I think they are in there having sex."

"No wonder they wanted the kids gone," she said with a smirk.

"Let's give them thirty minutes, then I'm coming back."

"We can stick the kids in the dining room for now." She looked over at the toddler balancing at the top of the stairs. "Shit!" She ran and grabbed it by the arm before it toppled headfirst down the stairs.

My heart skipped a beat.

"I'll take this one down," she said and started down the stairs.

I knew where the girl was, so I went to get her. I left her in the room with Megan. Madison was watching us with amusement. "Have you seen the boy?" I asked her.

She shook her head but pointed to my private drawing room. He was playing hide and seek? I went over there and opened the door. I didn't see him. My computer was still open to the bookkeeping software I was using, and papers were all over my desk. The only place to hide was the other side of the couch, and under the desk, so I checked around the couch. Nothing. Then I tiptoed to my desk to check behind it. Bingo.

"Found you!" I declared. He giggled and scampered up. I happened to glance at my computer to see everything I'd been working on was erased. My heart nearly stopped. I closed my eyes for a second and looked again. I was going to kill their parents.

Chapter Eleven

"Let's go," I said to the boy, and he followed me out. I left him with Megan in the dining room. She was organizing a game of go fish complete with snacks. I raced back to my books to try and restore the missing files. If I had to recreate everything, I was doomed. Luckily, everything, except for what I entered today, was backed up. It was still a couple of hours of work I had to redo, but the relief almost made it worth it. I re-entered it, finished up, saved, and shut the computer down. Then, because I'd obviously failed to lock the door when I left before, I locked the door and went out to check on Megan.

In my panic, I'd forgotten to go get the parents in thirty minutes, so Megan was obviously annoyed at me. I'd stuck her with the kids for almost two hours, and she looked ready to kill. I had her gather them all up. This time, I took the crew up the elevator. I wasn't sure it was a good idea showing kids how to operate it, but it was the only way I could think to contain them while traveling to the top of the house.

I knocked on the door. This time, it opened after a few seconds. "Yes?" Mrs. Nishiyama said.

"I'm very sorry, mam, but we don't run a daycare here. Your children need to be supervised at all times." I gestured for them to go inside. They did. Win for me.

She frowned at me. "Why weren't they supervised?"

"We don't offer childcare services and don't have the staff for it. *You* need to supervise them," I clarified.

"Oh, I'm very sorry. We just needed a few minutes alone."

I wasn't feeling very generous. "Then I suggest when you take children on a vacation, bring a nanny and get them their own room. While you're here, they need to be with one or both of you." Then I turned and headed back to the elevator. I wanted out of reach of her stare as soon as possible. When the door shut behind me, I nearly collapsed. I didn't do confrontations well. And with guests, I was horrified I'd get a bad review.

"How did it go?" Megan was behind the desk with Madison, getting ready to change shifts.

"I basically had to yell at her to watch her own kids."

She scoffed. "You never yell."

"Yeah? Well, I wanted to. I did have to speak sternly, and you know how I hate to do that."

"Yeah. Hopefully, that will be it, and they'll be perfectly behaved the rest of the time."

"I'll be surprised."

"I think I'd better study up on kitsunes and their culture," Megan said. "This isn't going well."

"Thanks. That's a good idea. I do feel like I'm missing something."

"It's never boring around here," Madison added. "As

long as no vamps are involved, I can stand guest shenanigans." She chuckled at her own joke.

I groaned. "Let's pray there are no vamps involved. I'm hoping that their latest flop is enough to send them back to eastern Europe with their tails between their legs."

"So do I, but do we have plans if they don't?" Madison asked.

I had nothing. I was burned out on supernatural war and being targeted for no other reason than I was powerful.

"We need some kind of early warning system, or a huge ward like the witches had," Megan added.

"Yeah, I wish I knew how to make one." The Fae didn't have wards, not like the witches. They could make barriers and such, but for some reason, either their magic wasn't conducive, or they'd never developed the technology to create a basic ward around somewhere.

If anyone could develop it, it would be Dana, who'd shown incredible magic expertise and the ability to invent based on an idea. I needed to give her this idea and see what she could do. I could block some spells depending on the elements thrown at me, and I could hide someone in shadows to the point they were invisible. There had to be a way to combine that into something more permanent. Too bad I was a beginner, without a lot of magic theory behind me. I sighed. "We'll have to rely on tech."

"What do we have besides cameras?" Megan asked.

"Nothing."

"Oh, maybe we should hire some guards," Megan said.

"We have Mr. Mittens, Goch and Brightfeather," I said.

She gave me a sour look. "Mr. Mittens covers the entire property; he can't be everywhere. Goch is usually gone realm walking, and Brightfeather just had babies. We don't have anyone."

I sighed; it was all true. Mr. Mittens would be hard to live with if I brought in some guards, and he'd probably sulk and punish me, but we needed something.

"Maybe Sorcha could send someone our way." Sorcha was my baincallan friend from Faerie, and she was a warrior. The idea seemed brilliant even to me.

"Huh, that does sound like a good idea."

"When do you want to go?" I thought for a minute. "There's time after the lunch service, and you know I can time walk, so whenever!"

"I'm going," Megan announced. Besides the kitsune family, the other guests were gone.

"I can stay an extra hour," Madison said. "But next time, I wanna see Faerie."

"Deal."

Megan looked down. "Should we change?"

"Yeah, probably."

We both went to our respective rooms and changed into Faerie robes. I called to Mr. Mittens because he would hate me if I left him out.

He wandered in as I was tying the last ties on my shimmering, iridescent blue robe.

I can see you are headed to Faerie, he said drolly.

"Yes. We need help keeping watch over this place. It's too big for just you."

He bristled visibly—his fur puffing out and his eyes narrowing. *I'm your protector.*

"You are. No one doubts that. However, we need to keep watch over the entire property to make sure we aren't invaded by vamps again. I thought I'd ask Sorcha and the Scáthanna if they would hire out a few *baincallan* for patrol and protection. I need you to judge their ability. You in?"

I know what you are doing. He licked a snow-white mitten.

"What am I doing?"

Manipulating me so I won't be annoyed at you.

"Is it working?"

Of course. He put his paw down. *I will go.*

"Splendid. We'll go as soon as Megan comes down."

Hmpf.

I met Megan at the base of the stairs. Madison knew where we were going, and since I could walk us back to this moment, I didn't think to text Gabe or Luke that we were leaving. I looked around to memorize the time so I could walk back to this moment. I grasped Megan's hand and the three of us walked.

Chapter Twelve

Unlike the last time I plunked us down in Faerie, I knew where I was going and how to get there. We landed outside of my grandfather's den in his keep. Since it was incredibly dangerous to surprise him, I knocked on the study door. I didn't know if he was even home; he could be at court or out putting down an uprising.

"Enter," his voice boomed out.

I opened the door, and Megan, Mr. Mittens, and I wandered in.

His eyebrows shot up. "What did I do to deserve this lovely visit?" He must be in a great mood.

"Umm, we just wanted to say hi?" I said lamely. I should visit more often instead of only showing when I needed something.

He laughed. "You aren't the best at deceit, grand-daughter."

True. The myth that the Fae couldn't lie wasn't really accurate. They couldn't directly lie, but they made deceit an art form.

"I came to beg the king for a few baincallan guards. The woods are too large for just Mr. Mittens to patrol for vampires."

My grandfather stared at Mr. Mittens; I was sure they were conversing privately. He looked back up at me. "I see." He stood and walked around. Pacing was how he thought. "I believe that a few can be spared."

My grandfather was the high king's Pendragon—leader of all his armies. He could authorize the release of a few guards to me, although it would be best to go through the king, since his mistress was the captain of the Scáthanna— the king's elite baincallan guard.

"I believe six would be a good force. Let me speak with the king."

"I appreciate your help, Grandfather."

He gestured for us to join him by the fire. We sat in the comfortable chairs he kept there for visiting. Before he sat, he pulled the rope that signaled his servants. Soon, a familiar man in my grandfather's livery appeared in the door.

"Please send word to the king that I seek an audience soon on a personal matter."

"Yes, milord."

And now we waited. Mr. Mittens jumped into my lap and begged for ear scritches. He was such a goofball some- times. We all knew he could shift into Fae form here, but he liked to play housecat when it suited him—and it always suited him to get pets.

"Xrsrphn, please show some restraint," my grandfather reprimanded.

Mr. Mittens opened one glowing blue eye, and then closed it. He rolled over on his back, all four legs splayed wide to get belly rubs. I complied.

My grandfather sighed. I did realize he had a different relationship than I had with my cat, but something in their past had left Mr. Mittens with a geas to protect my grandfather's line. I think the only way he could show his displeasure was to play the role of domestic cat to the extreme.

I didn't mind. To me, he was my beloved cat first, protector second. Of course to him, I was his pet first, my protector second. It worked for us.

"I saved your court clothing," my grandfather said. He must have been noticing our daily Fae robes.

"We'll go change," I said, taking the hint. Megan and I headed to the rooms we had here and changed. I had several dresses that were court ready. I chose a fire-colored dress to match my hair, and Megan chose a green one. There wasn't a way to do fancy Fae court hair, that actually required someone to do it for you, but I brushed mine and it let it hang in waves.

We finished quickly and headed back down to the den. Mr. Mittens stayed behind. He wasn't well loved at court, and he wanted to nap.

It must have been a slow day at court because it wasn't more than an hour before we had a response.

"Milord, the king has approved your visit. You may attend the court."

My grandfather looked at me. "Shall we?"

We headed to his transporter room and piled in. Grandfather spoke the word that transferred us to the palace. We exited the white room into a gleaming white hallway. We followed my grandfather through several twisting corridors and different floors until we stood before the towering doors into the throne room.

I felt a little anxiety. The last time I was here had been quite stressful. I'd been prepared to marry the king, against my will, and then my grandfather and I had been arrested for treason. All of that had been cleared up, thanks to our efforts to reveal the true threat, but it had left me with lasting emotional scars.

My grandfather informed the servant guarding the doors, and a few moments later we were ushered in and announced. I gulped and looked around. Full court. Many people knew me and knew about me. They looked on me with pity, like I was the scorned bride. I guess they didn't know I was the scorner. I wanted to yell, "I have a boyfriend," to the gathered crowds. But it would have meant nothing to them.

We approached the throne. The king sat, his golden hair brushing his shoulders, his perfect Fae face set at bemused. Diamin, the captain of the king's guard, sat in the queen's seat. I wondered if they had already married, but it hadn't been that long I thought—although time passed oddly between our two realms. It could have been longer or shorter than I remembered.

"Greetings, dear Pendragon," the king said.

Grandfather bowed his head, and Megan and I curtsied.

The king acknowledged us with a look. But he didn't address us. I guess that wasn't done to your ex.

"I've come to request a team of six of your baincallan guards for a special assignment."

The king frowned slightly.

"From my Scáthanna?"

"Yes, sire."

The king leaned over to talk to his mate. She was in two-legged form, but when she was acting captain, she'd appear in her centaur form—or baincallan as they preferred to be called.

68

She also frowned and said something back.

"My queen-to-be will assemble a group."

"You are most benevolent, sire." My grandfather inclined his head in gratitude.

With that, we were dismissed and walked out of the court.

As we hurried back to the transporter room, Megan asked, "When's the wedding?"

"In a fortnight," Grandfather answered.

"How are the Fae taking having a baincallan as a queen?" I remembered the court gossip when they were just having an affair, and it hadn't been flattering.

"You want court gossip?" my grandfather asked with a laugh.

"Well, I did get used to hearing it."

"I don't know. It won't matter soon enough. She'll be queen, and everyone will hold their tongues."

I shrugged. I guessed it wasn't my business anymore, so I let it go. "When do you think he'll send over the guards?" I asked.

"I assume it will be done fairly quickly. No more than a day."

A day? I was in a hurry. I knew I could time walk home, but it just felt like a huge delay. Anything could be happening at home, and I wasn't there. I wondered if we should just go home and then come back to transport the new guards.

"Meg, do you want to go home and come back?" I asked her.

She shrugged. "I want to say hi to Dana first."

Megan had a much better relationship with Dana than I did. Dana liked my plucky human friend. She found me barely adequate but felt compelled to help me since she was my grandfather's mistress of magic and had a serious crush on him.

I'd told him about the crush, but I don't know if anything had happened. Nothing from what I could tell. At least the king had taken my advice. Maybe that was why Diamin let me take some of her soldiers. Huh.

When we returned to Grandfather's keep, Megan and I excused ourselves to find Dana. When she wasn't with my grandfather, she was in her lab. So that's where we headed.

Sure enough, she was working on a project. We knocked gently; you didn't want to startle someone who might be working on something that went boom.

"Dana?" I said softly.

"Just a minute," she snapped.

So, we stood quietly and waited. She finished whatever she was doing, whispered words over it, then turned around.

"Hmmm. Already need more fireballs?"

"No, we were visiting and thought we'd say hi," I said, lamely.

"Hey, Dana, what are you working on?" Megan added.

"Another idea. Explosive fire magic."

"That's cool."

She peered at Megan. "Have you been practicing with your spear?"

"Every day."

I looked at Megan. I didn't know that. "When do you do that?"

She shrugged. "Before you get up. Mr. Mittens helps out."

"He does?" Even my cat had a secret life. He helped me practice at the waterfall, but I didn't know he also helped Megan.

"He sometimes will attack me, so I have someone to fight."

"You aren't afraid of stabbing him?"

"I was, but I rarely even touch him, so it's fine. I'm getting better, though."

"Are you ready to start training with the sword?" Dana asked.

"Yes," she said quickly. I knew my friend had taken to combat, but she had way more confidence than I did.

"I can arrange to come by and begin teaching you, but you'll have to stay here after you learn the basics to train."

"I look forward to it."

Dana held up a magic ball. "This is your sword; you need a new magic word."

Megan tilted her head and thought. "Holy hand grenade."

Dana whispered over the ball and handed it to Megan. "Go ahead and activate it."

Megan said her new phrase, and the magic ball burst into a long silvery sword. "Sweet!" She lunged, thrusting the sword forward, and then swiping it back and forth. When she was done, she spoke her phrase, and the sword collapsed back into a marble. She dropped it into her pocket.

"You are amazing, Dana." Megan said, careful not to thank the half-Fae.

Dana beamed. I had the feeling more than once that she didn't get praised often. She deserved it, though.

Dana turned a less than thrilled eye to me. "What do you want? I know it wasn't just to say hello."

I sighed. I did want to say hello, and I didn't want a lot, just to ask a question. "We came to get some guards to help us against the vampires. However, I did have a thought and a challenge for you if you're willing to give it a try?"

I figured appealing to her vanity would be helpful. She was very proud of her abilities, rightly so.

She stiffened. "What new impossible task have you dreamed up?"

I wanted to smile. She'd met my impossible ideas so far. "I was wondering if you could build a magical shield large enough to protect my house?"

She frowned. She didn't understand. I looked around for something to use to give her a visual. I saw a crystal glass on her worktable. It had some water in it. I dumped the water in the sink and had Megan hand me her new magic ball. "Pretend this is my house." I set the marble down on the worktable. "This glass is a shield." I placed the glass upside down over the magic ball. Then I flicked the glass, and it rang with a lovely bell sound. "Now, I can't get to the house. It's protected."

Dana stared at my demo. I could see the cogs spinning in between her ears. The Fae didn't have wards; they'd never developed them. It was pointless when magic abounded. Someone would always get through, but on earth, magic was rare and weak. It would be an amazing feat to develop a strong ward that could protect the house from vampires.

"It would need a door?" Dana asked.

"It would need to let authorized individuals in and out of it."

Now she frowned deeper. "Impossible."

"You activate your magic balls with a word all the time. Couldn't you make it respond to a word?"

She stared at me, then back at her table. "Leave me, I need to think."

I lifted the glass, gave Megan back her sword ball, and

we left. It didn't pay to anger Dana. She would definitely smite us.

Once the door shut behind us, Megan said, "You love to challenge her, don't you?"

I smiled. "Yeah, but only because I think she's amazing and can do more if someone has the imagination to push her harder."

"She is pretty awesome."

"Yeah, but she likes you. She only tolerates me. I'm trying to stay on her good side. If I keep her busy, she'll forget to torture me."

"She likes you, too."

I laughed.

"She really does."

We decided to stay the night. My impatience was my own, and time travel made it possible to not be late getting home.

Chapter Thirteen

The next morning, true to the king's word, six baincallan warriors arrived via the transporter room. They gathered in the courtyard with their weapons and gear. My grandfather called us down to meet them.

"Sorcha!" I greeted my friend, who was part of the group.

She smiled. "Brigid, it is great to see you."

Sorcha had been my personal guard when I'd been the king's intended bride. It had taken me a while to break through her shell, but she'd helped us save the king at great risk to herself.

"Were you ordered, or did you get to choose?" I asked, guilt filling me. I didn't think about the guards themselves. I was as bad as the rulers in this land.

"No, we were given the choice. Diamin is a good leader."

"I'm so glad you chose to come! I'll get to show you my home and my realm!"

She led me over to the rest of the group. "This is Brigid. We'll be traveling to her realm."

I had a sudden thought, and it was a doozy. "There isn't a lot of magic in my realm. I have a link to Faerie, and it helps. How will that affect you?" I remembered that she'd told me once that the baincallan were made from magic. I didn't know what that meant for them.

She thought for a moment. "We don't need magic for anything but a boost when we shift from four legs to two legs."

I thought about what any non-supernatural would think if they saw the baincallan in their preferred form. They had the torso of a human woman, and the rest of them was horse. They were tall and distinctive, and most humans would immediately know them as centaurs.

Sorcha read my face. "We have been training in both forms. Diamin saw that benefit during the attempted coup. We can shift to two legs here."

She barked out orders to her group, and they dropped their gear and shifted to two legs.

"We'll need a moment to switch our armor. No sense taking both sets if we only need one."

That seemed practical. They shifted their gear, and the servants found somewhere to store the unneeded equipment. While they readied themselves, I said goodbye to my grandfather. Megan was training with Dana, so I left her to it and started transporting baincallan to my house.

I brought Sorcha and three others with me. I left them in the parking lot. I hadn't really prepared a place for barracks. I'd thought I'd put them up in the stables because I was thinking they would be in centaur form. Now, I needed to prepare better quarters. The dairy house was out. Jim and Chef Jack already shared that with two hands. There was an unused building that had been cleared out. Before I went back to retrieve the others, I called Jim, and gave him the info and set him to the task of housing my new troops. It'd be rough for a few days, but I'd have them beds and whatever else they needed soon.

Maybe the Whelans would have time to fix it up. I'd ask once I came back with Megan, Mr. Mittens, and the rest of the baincallan. I told Sorcha I'd be right back and walked.

When we arrived back, seconds later, Sorcha had a kitsune laying at her feet, her sword to its throat.

Since the fox had three tails, and was adult sized, I assumed it was one of the parents. I wasn't gone long enough for this!

"Sorcha, please remove your sword. The fox is one of my guests."

She lifted it slightly. "This fox was trying to sneak into the house."

"It's OK. It is staying here. I run an inn."

She lifted the sword with a frown.

I'd better fill them in a lot better on what we wanted them to guard against. I didn't want any scared or dead guests. First, to get them settled.

"Megan, I'm going to run them over to the dairy. Are you good for a while over here?"

It was her turn to take over for Madison. I checked my watch. The time walking was spot on. I'd only lost a few moments in transition.

"Sure, I'm gonna change, and then I'll relieve her."

"Thanks!"

I had the two-legged baincallan follow me on foot to the other side of the property. It was late April, and usually, this was a rainy time of year. But the sun was out, and everything was glorious. Even the mud had receded, and the ground was soft and nearly dry. We took the trail through the woods. Mr. Mittens led the way. He still didn't like me to wander around the property without him, although six fierce Fae warriors should be good enough to protect me.

How are you going to explain to them what they are guarding against? he asked me as we walked.

"I thought you'd do it. This is your team," I said with a smile.

He paused. One paw raised, and he swung his fuzzy head around to stare at me. *Hmpf.*

I laughed. "I figured I'd show them some of the footage from the exterior cameras so they can see what vampires look like and what they can turn into to start."

That seems a more acceptable option. You should also introduce them to all the standard and accepted members that live on the property.

"I agree. We'll start with Jim and Chef Jack."

We left the shelter of the woods and walked out to the gate to the furthest paddock. A few cows basked in the sun, calmly chewing their cud. We didn't even get a curious head swing. I also had a few sheep and goats for hungry carnivores.

"What are these creatures?" Sorcha asked.

When she'd been here before, she'd only had time to fight against a Fae army and hadn't had time to explore. "The larger black and white creature we call a cow. They are placid, and we can get milk from them, which we can make into cheese, cream, butter, and ice cream. As for the fuzzy white animals with black heads, those are sheep. We harvest their hair to make cloth. The other animals with horns are goats. We also use them for milk and cheese."

"We also have milk, cheese, and cream on Faerie, and we also use animals. What is ice cream?"

Oh my, was she in for a treat. My eyes lit up with happiness. To introduce someone to ice cream for the first time would be a true delight.

"It's wonderful. Think of it as flavored frozen cream."

"Is this something you devised with your ice magic?" Sorcha asked.

I laughed. "No, but I wish I'd invented it. It's been around for a long time."

"Hmm."

We cleared three more fields and walked onto the gravel of the dairy. Jim was waiting for us, leaning against his side-by-side, farm tools thrown in.

"Sorcha and ladies, this is Jim. He's my farm manager. I hate to say that I didn't have a place prepared for you, but he's going to have it up and running within the next three days. If you don't mind it a little rough for a bit, we'll have a nice barracks for you."

Jim led us to the empty building. It had originally been a storage facility for feed and equipment. But we'd built a new up-to-date facility for that. I'd intended to expand and add this building with more stalls. It was currently empty. We'd cleaned it and painted the walls, but it was basically a cement slab with walls and a roof. There wasn't a bathroom. It was early enough in the day that I could have some porta potties delivered. There was a shower in the stables, so that would do until I could get one installed in this building. I also had some old cots I'd purchased from an army navy outlet once, thinking I'd need them for workers, but never did. I'd have Jim bring those in.

I texted Megan to call and get two porta potties sent over.

We walked in. "I'm sorry, it's basic."

"This is sufficient." Sorcha shrugged.

"Jim will bring you cots, and I'll show you where you can shower. I'm having toilets brought over for you."

The baincallan dumped their gear against a wall and followed me over to the stables, where I showed them the shower room.

I started thinking about everything I needed to do to prepare my guards and figured I'd need to take a run to town to pick up some additional equipment. I needed a way to show them all the video I had of our fight with the vampires. I figured I'd get a large TV. They might enjoy it for the barracks as well.

"Get settled. I'll come back and get you in about three hours? Is that enough time?"

"It is more than enough," Sorcha answered.

By the time we were back at the new barracks, Jim was already hauling in cots. The women set them up quickly. I noticed an issue almost immediately. The baincallan were tall. They were taller than most earth men. All of them were between six foot six to seven feet tall and proportionately large. Amazonian really. The cots were a little short. I apologized. But the baincallan didn't seem bothered. They were also dressed for Faerie, not earth. As long as they stayed on the property, it wouldn't be a problem, but I should order at least one set of basic earth clothing for each of them. There had to be a big and tall store for women, right? The things I needed to do added up. I made my escape.

When Mr. Mittens and I walked into the kitchen, I realized I hadn't told Chef Jack about six very large women he needed to feed. That meant a lot more groceries. He gave me a list.

After that, I went to talk to Megan to see if she'd completed her tasks.

"Luke said he and Noah can probably get your barracks done in two days, if the lumber store has what they need. Oh, and the honey dippers are bringing two porta potties in an hour."

"You are the best!" I said. "I feel like I could have prepared better."

She shrugged. "Like you knew that vampires would come after us, and we'd need a private army."

"True."

"But I should have had the barracks done before we went to Faerie. I've asked Sorcha and her team to sacrifice for me. I feel sort of icky about it."

"Aren't you paying them?"

"Yeah."

"They're professionals. I'm sure they'll be happy with three meals and a place to lay their heads."

I hoped so. I should have been better prepared, and I felt like a terrible host.

Brigid!

A mental voice shocked me, and I jumped slightly.

"What's wrong?" Megan asked.

I shook my head, waiting for more of the message. It was so sudden; I wasn't sure who it was from.

Mr. Mittens came flying through the kitchen doors. I looked at him.

Two griffins have landed in the parking area. They are demanding that you come out, he said.

Great.

Chapter Fourteen

I didn't have time for a couple of privileged griffins who were only here to make problems. Megan and I followed Mr. Mittens out to the back porch. Chef Jack asked if we needed help, but I shook my head. I didn't really know yet.

Chef Jack was a weretiger and extremely dangerous. I didn't know if he could take two griffins, but between him, Mr. Mittens, and me, we might survive.

The two griffins were magnificent. One looked like Umber, Brightfeather's mate. It was snowy white with brown feathers interspersed, and tall ear-like feathers sprouting above an owl shaped head. Its front feet were the owl's talons, fluffy feathers covered its forelimbs all the way to the ground. The lion half was dark brown, and powerfully muscled, its long whiplike tail ending in a puff of black hair. It looked regal.

The other had a traditional eagle's head, but not a silvery one like Brightfeather. This one was more like a golden eagle. Brown and gold feathers on its eagle half, and tawny lion in the back.

Mr. Mittens jumped up on the porch railing, where he could observe and engage if needed. Megan and I approached, keeping a safe distance. Her hands were in her pockets, where I knew she fondled her magic balls.

"I'm Brigid," I said out loud. Both heads inclined slightly to me.

The owl griffin spoke. "I am Thorn, and my mate is Firial. We are the parents of the griffin Umber. We are here seeking him."

I should be prepared for this. But Brightfeather and I had both been busy and hadn't really prepared for this day. Umber had come here looking to reconnect with his mate and had lost his life in the middle of the vampire war.

"I have met him, briefly," I said.

"We have news for him, if you know where he is."

"I do not. He and his mate were reconciling. I haven't seen him for some time."

There, that wasn't a complete lie. I hadn't seen him, not since we'd buried him by the waterfall.

"If you do, would you please leave him the message to return home?" Firial said.

"Of course."

"Thank you."

I inclined my head, and they launched themselves into the sky, circled the house, and took off headed towards the highway, luckily.

I sagged with relief when they left. This wasn't good. I'd promised Brightfeather I'd help her keep her children a secret from her in-laws. But this was looking like something I was going to regret deeply.

"What are we going to do?" Megan asked after they were out of earshot.

I shook my head. I had no idea.

"They deserve to know that their son is dead."

"I know. It's just not my call. It's not my secret."

"I know. But they'll be back."

I sighed. "Yeah. I know I'd be. I guess I need to let Brightfeather know and check on her."

"I think you need to do that ASAP."

"I have a list of things I need to do." I sighed. It never ended. "I guess I should get this over with."

"Because you are so busy and stressed, you should know that Dana's coming in the morning to train. She said and I quote, 'Brigid should join us. She can barely keep herself alive.'"

I groaned. "What else is new?"

Megan shrugged. "It'll be fun."

Mr. Mittens decided to accompany me to Brightfeather's nest. I picked him up, and realm walked us there.

"Brightfeather?" I called out, so I didn't startle her.

In the nest, her tired voice answered in my head.

I should have been more help. She had to be busy feeding three hungry mouths.

Mr. Mittens and I entered her nest. The three griffinettes were sleeping, all huddled up like puppies in a pile.

I just got them to sleep. I was going to nap.

"I'm so sorry, but this couldn't wait. Umber's parents just stopped at the house."

That got her attention, and her head snapped up from its mossy bed. *What did they say? Do they know?* Her panic was slipping through her mental voice.

I shook my head. "They are looking for Umber. They said they had important news for him. I didn't know what to say, so I told them I hadn't seen him in a while. I was vague. They don't know about the hatchlings."

She gave an audible groan and laid her head back down. *I'm so tired. I can't think right now. Can you come back tomorrow? I need to come up with a plan. I need to tell them about Umber. I think we should prepare a story.*

"Yes, of course. I'll see if I can bring some meat for the little ones as well. Rest. I'm sure we'll have a few days before they come back."

Perhaps. Thanks for letting me know.

Her mental voice was so tired that Mr. Mittens and I slipped out. I could hear her steady breath as she fell asleep before we were all the way out of the nest.

We walked back to the house. I went to grab my bag and car keys to go run my errands. My keys were missing. I always kept them clipped to my handbag, and since I ran a public inn, I kept my purse locked in my private suite.

I had walked right in. The door hadn't been locked. I stopped. Had I forgotten to lock it? That wasn't like me.

I dumped my purse on the bed. I needed to check if everything was there. Maybe I'd dropped my keys inside.

Mints, lip gloss, spare mascara, wallet—everything in its place, compact mirror, sharpie, two pens, a couple of pony-tail holders, brush, mini-lint roller for Mr. Mitten fuzz, and a half a chocolate bar. Everything seemed to be there, with the exception of my keys. I put everything back, and walked out, purse over my shoulder. I locked my door and checked it. Locked.

Megan was scrolling through her phone at the desk.

"Did I leave my keys here?" I asked.

"I'll look." She checked the drawers and shelves behind the desk. "Not here."

"Huh. I'll check my desk."

I also kept the private drawing room slash office locked when I wasn't in there. They were off limits to guests. I tried the door, and it too was unlocked. I knew I wouldn't forget both. Something was fishy.

Chapter Fifteen

I'm not proud that I automatically assumed it was the kitsune family. They'd been the guests trying my patience this round. Part of me wanted to grab the fox kits and shake them until my keys fell out, but that wasn't a guarantee.

Instead, I took a deep breath and texted poor Madison, who would have just barely made it home.

"Madison, did you happen to see anyone lingering around my bedroom or drawing room earlier?"

Meanwhile, I searched through my desk drawer for my spare car fob. I hadn't even used it yet, not since buying the car, and I vaguely remembered dropping it into the drawer. It was hidden under some papers. I pulled it out in triumph as my text tone sounded.

"The family wandered out a few times and back, but the only person I saw hanging around your bedroom door was the psychic."

My eyebrows shot up in surprise. That was interesting. "Thanks."

"Why did something happen?"

"My doors were unlocked, and my keys were missing. It's probably nothing. Don't worry!"

Did psychics have other powers like magical lock picks? I guess if I had to, I could bend my magic to opening a lock, more than likely I'd blast apart the door before I was finished, but I could open a locked door. Oh well, I'd have to worry about it after I picked up the extra supplies on my list.

Spare key fob and purse securely in hand, I headed out.

Before I returned home, I had a text from Luke. They had everything and would come by tonight to start the barracks. I breathed a sigh of relief. One thing off my plate. I'd have to let Sorcha know as soon as I was back.

I pulled onto my long, now paved, driveway. The stretch through the woods and up a slight incline immediately put a smile on my face. I loved my home. I loved the power I felt sing through me when I entered the small little slice of Faerie on earth. It wasn't as rich in magic as the Fae realm, but it was still richer than anywhere else I'd been on earth.

A fox darted across the road in front of me, and I slammed on the brakes. Packages slid and plastic crinkled in the back. I flinched. I didn't like to hit anything living, but this fox had two tails, so I knew it was one of my Kitsune guests. I really didn't want to hit one of them.

The fox stopped on the edge of the road and glared at me. It was human part of the time. It had to know how to look both ways before crossing the street. I almost leaned my head out of the window to say that, but I just waved and continued up the drive.

I parked as close as I could to the kitchen door, while still staying out of teen dragon landing range. I gathered up my purchases and deposited them on the old kitchen table. Chef Jack went out to get the rest. I thanked him. He was hugely strong and came in with all the rest, although it would have taken me three more trips.

He laughed when I told him that. Weretiger humor I supposed.

I left him to it and headed to the front desk. I figured I should check in with Megan before I went to check on Sorcha to set up the TV and give them their directions.

Megan was scrolling through her phone.

"Boring up front?" I asked casually.

"Mind numbing," she replied, but didn't put down her phone.

"Did you print the pictures of the guests?"

She put down her phone and handed me a sheaf of papers. "Yeah. Although I was tempted to throw out the pics of the kitsunes. I'd love for the baincallan to take out the adults. They've been severely annoying."

I sighed. "What happened?" So far, their shenanigans were just like Megan pointed out, annoying. But they hadn't done anything unforgivable like my first guest had by bringing in a poltergeist.

"Just underfoot, constant questions, being places they shouldn't, complaining, you name it."

"Thought it was mind numbingly boring up here?" I joked.

She rolled her eyes. "It is, and in between, the kitsunes drive me nuts."

"Yeah, I had to slam on my brakes when one crossed in front of my car on the way up the drive."

"How many tails?"

"Two, why?"

"That's the oldest kid. I've been reading up on them. They gain tails with age and wisdom." She shrugged.

"Wisdom, huh?" I guess none of them had more than three tails then. I laughed to myself.

"I know, go figure." She snorted.

Just then, the mom strolled in. I'd have to look up their names soon. I was horrible with names. I kept having to look them up. Megan knew it, though, and looked at the papers in my hands. Right. I was holding that info. I checked. Tomiko Nishiyama.

"How can I help you, Mrs. Nishiyama?" I asked.

"We need more towels."

"I'll bring them right up."

"I can take them. I'm standing right here."

"One moment."

I hurried to the laundry area where we kept the spare linens and grabbed five towels. They couldn't need more than that, could they?

"Here you go. Do I need to come and pick up the soiled towels?"

"No."

OK, no explanation, huh? Maybe the maid grabbed them earlier and forgot to replace them. I'd speak to her when she came in tomorrow. Or better yet, I'd check if she left any notes.

The woman marched up the stairs. Odd. Sort of rude as well.

Once she was at the top, Megan said, "See what I mean?"

I nodded. "Did the maid leave any notes?"

"Yup. They wouldn't let her in to clean the room, and when she knocked, they told her to go away."

"Great. Hope that doesn't mean I'll be cleaning crayon off the walls."

"Or worse."

Oh well, I couldn't worry about it now. "I'm going to drive around to the dairy. I have a TV and other items to drop off at the new barracks. Plus, a brief." I waved the papers.

"Have fun."

"Yeah, a laugh riot."

I headed out the back kitchen door and turned to my car. The TV and some earth clothing for the baincallan were in the back. I was focused on it and didn't notice Mr. Mittens until he was nearly in front of me. He was in his Splintercat form, and he had a squiggling fox kit in his mouth.

I groaned.

This creature was headed up the trail to the waterfall, he announced, annoyance in his voice.

The kit only had one tail, so I knew it was one of the smaller children, both girls. I took the kit from his mouth. It shifted, and the toddler, much heavier than the fox, almost slipped from my hands. It began to wail.

"Thanks for keeping it safe," I said. "I didn't realize they could find the trail, so I'll have to put up a sign and announce that they aren't allowed up there."

Hmpf was his only reply.

Plus, I'd just spoken to the parents about watching out for their own children. Now, their toddler was roaming the property alone. There were honest to goodness predators that lived on my land. This little one was a perfect snack size for an eagle or an owl to scoop up. And that was just normal earth creatures. The magic in this place called to supernatural creatures from this realm and others as well.

Mr. Mittens shrank back to his Ragdoll form and wandered away. This place was a lot for one cat to patrol. I dumped the child on the front desk, and it was time for Megan to sigh.

"What did we do to deserve this?"

"I don't know, but we definitely pissed off a god or something."

She laughed. "Yeah."

I left again. This time, I made it to the car and started down the drive.

Chapter Sixteen

Jim met me at the barracks, and as usual, quietly unloaded the car and had the TV set up before I could offer him help. The baincallan watched me curiously. They had no idea what the rectangular monstrosity was.

I plugged it in and booted it up.

Sorcha walked up to me and touched the screen. "What is this?"

"Do you remember the recording device?"

When I'd gone to Faerie the first time, Dana had devised a device to record sound and visuals for playback. It had helped us uncover the plot to kill the king.

Her face scrunched up. "This is much bigger and doesn't have wings."

I laughed. "You are correct. It is only for sound and video, not for recording. I'm going to show you a recording I made of vampires so that you can know what you are guarding against. Can you explain this to them?" I tilted my head at the five other baincallan.

"I will try."

She turned and started explaining. I worked on connecting my phone to the TV.

Once I was done, I passed along the papers on my current guests. "These are the guests staying this week at the inn. They are authorized to be there. Also, the staff pictures are in there. You've met Jim and Megan."

I pulled out the bags of clothes. "I thought you might like to dress more like the local population, so I brought some clothes." I handed out leggings and t-shirts. "They are comfortable. I wasn't sure of your sizes, but I figured you can sort that out." I handed the bags of extras to Sorcha. I pinched the leg of my leggings and pulled it out to show the stretch. "You'll love these."

Sorcha set down the bag of spares and picked up her pair of leggings. She'd ended up with a pair that was black with colorful flowers. I figured the prints would act like camouflage in the woods.

She stripped off her clothes. I stared in shock. No underwear in Faerie, apparently. I should have realized. I'd have to buy some, if only for my own peace of mind. She tried to put them on backwards until I showed them all the writing goes in the back. She pulled them on. Then the t-shirt. She immediately dropped into a deep crouch and kicked out with her long legs. Then she sprinted in place with high knees. When she was done, she nodded. "Lots of give. They are adequate."

With all the women changed, it looked like I was hosting a WNBA team in my outbuilding instead of escapees from Paradise Island.

"OK, gather round. I'm going to start the recording."

The women sat cross-legged in front of the TV. I started the video I had cued up. Immediately, the women reeled back in fear from the sounds and images on the screen.

I stopped the video.

"It's OK, this isn't real. It's a replay of things that happened three months ago. It can't hurt you."

I invited them all to come up and feel the screen with the images frozen on them. They did, murmuring in surprise. Once they settled again, I started the video.

This time, they watched warily but weren't as surprised. I paused it a few times to explain what they were seeing. "This is a vampire in human form." I paused it. The vamp had his mouth open, fangs showing. "This is a typical shifted vampire in bat form." I did this for all the old vamp forms as well, then restarted the video to talk about how to dispatch them. We watched it several times at the request of the baincallan. I pointed out the Whelans, Gabe, and Chef Jack and Jim in shifted form. They hadn't met any of them except Gabe in the battle against the Fae and Sofia.

Once all was settled, Sorcha and I talked over a guard rotation schedule. I gave her a topographic map of my property to use and a cell phone. That took a minute to explain. I showed the baincallan how to use the TV to watch other movies and videos from the internet. That didn't go well, and I doubted they'd know how to work it after I left. I put the TV on a documentary about North American animals and left. Sorcha would take it from here. Luke and the Whelans would be in tomorrow to fix up the barracks. All was well.

I climbed in my car and drove slowly around the building to the road. Before I went far, Jim waved me down. I rolled down my window.

"Hi, what's up?"

Jim wasn't a big talker, so it must be important. "The kelpie is staying in the pond, so don't bring anyone to fish."

We'd already decided that, so I frowned at him. "Why? We'd already decided that?" I was curious.

"You didn't send the kids over to fish?"

I closed my eyes. The kitsunes again. How did they have enough time to cause this much trouble?

"I did not. Thanks for letting me know. I'll talk to the parents again." I was seriously considering asking them to leave. But they hadn't done anything past mischievous yet.

Before I left, I figured I'd better check on my other guests. "Any issues on this side?"

"No. Model customers so far. I just don't want to tempt fate."

"Understandable, and I appreciate that."

He gave me a slight tip of his hat, and I drove away.

Chapter Seventeen

I felt like going on the warpath, but when I pulled back up and parked in my spot, I saw Gabe's car and the immediate warmth that filled me melted away the anger. I popped out of my vehicle with a definite lightness in my feet. I almost twirled before I entered through the back door. I waved at Jack and continued to the front.

The smile that greeted me was the one he reserved for me. I threw my arms around him. He picked me up off the floor in a hug, and since it was only Megan, he followed that up with a smoking hot kiss.

"Good afternoon, gorgeous," he said once he put me down.

"Back at you."

"Are you busy?" he asked.

There were a ton of things to be done, as usual, but nothing that had to be done this instant. The baincallan were now on the job, and everything I could do for them was done or set up. The kitsune were more annoying than dangerous, and I had no proof the psychic had really stolen my keys. Plus, what would she do with them? Steal my car? That would be obvious. It had to be the kitsune kits being mischievous.

"No, I'm free for a while. What do you have in mind?"

"I thought I'd take you to dinner and ask you out for Saturday night for a concert in town."

"That sounds amazing. Give me a few minutes to freshen up." I'm sure after traveling to Faerie, dealing with the griffins, taking care of the baincallan, I needed more than simple freshening. I probably needed hosing down. "Maybe you'd better give me thirty minutes."

"That's fine. I'll hang out with Megan, but before you go, here." He grabbed a bag off the floor and handed it to me.

I looked inside and laughed. It was a walkie talkie set. We had a set when we were kids that we used back before cell phones that weren't super expensive bricks. One thing about Gabe, he was a romantic. I'd had every bit of romance in my body destroyed by my ex. Luckily, Gabe was bringing it back. I opened the set and handed him his. We both put in our batteries.

"This set has a range of ten miles. So you can talk to me when we're both at home."

I laughed again. We talked every night before bed. "I see you splurged for the expensive set."

"Anything for you."

I couldn't stop giggling. This was almost the exact conversation we'd had twenty something years ago. I kissed him and took my walkie talkie with me into the bathroom to get ready.

This was why I loved him. My ex would have...no. I wasn't going to think about Evan. He was not my problem anymore. I had to let go of all the insecurities he'd left me with. I was doing great, and Gabe, well… Gabe was as close to perfect as I would ever find.

I took a very fast shower. I couldn't usually do that because of the time it took to do my hair, but I washed it, and just braided it wet in one long French braid down my back. When done, I called him on the walkie. "Almost ready, over!"

"Can't wait, over," Gabe replied.

I brushed on some mascara and lip gloss and called it good. I dressed in a pair of snug jeans and a blue top that brought out my eyes. I was ready in thirty minutes. I kind of wanted to pat myself on the back for that.

"Wow! I'm shocked you really did that in thirty," Megan said, checking her phone for the time, smirking at me as I left my room and locked it behind me.

"Ha ha. I can be fast when I'm motivated."

"He is a big hunk of motivation," she said, giving him a measured look.

"He is," I agreed.

"He is also standing here," Gabe added.

We laughed.

"I'm ready." I announced, although it was clear since I was standing there with my bag, fully dressed.

Gabe held out his elbow, and I slipped my hand in. He led me to the kitchen since he was parked by me in the back. Chef Jack gave us a wave, and then we exited. As we stepped onto the porch, we were met by Mr. Mittens.

Will you be gone long? he asked.

I almost answered, but then narrowed my eyes. He didn't ever ask about my plans, unless…

"Why?"

He jumped up on his favorite perch, the railing around the porch, and stared into my eyes. *There is an issue.*

I groaned and rolled my eyes. Gabe stiffened and dropped my arm. After the vamps and everything else, we were immediately on edge.

Gabe looked around, checking the surroundings and the sky. When you had griffins, dragons, and vampire bats dropping in on you, it was always a good idea to look up.

"What is it?"

An incursion.

I looked at him thoughtfully. He generally told me *after* he'd killed whatever had shown up unannounced. Now he was acting nonchalant, if tense, and telling me about it. What did that mean?

"Spit it out. You're making me nervous. What has you disturbed?"

As I said it, I realized it was true. He was bothered. Either that meant that it was something that scared him, or something that he thought I'd be mad about if he killed.

He looked away. Damn. Something he thought he should kill but didn't think I would.

"Well?"

There is a unicorn foal in the woods by the spring, he finally said.

I'd had one run-in with a unicorn. They were major assholes. My first thought was to kill them all, but a foal? How bad could one baby hell horse be?

"A foal?"

Yes. It is very young.

"Where is its mother?"

I was waiting for an "I don't know" or "It fell through a portal" but he looked away, ashamed.

"You killed it."

Yes. I didn't know it had a foal. It was hidden.

I sighed. None of us would have suffered a unicorn to

99

live here. However, we weren't monsters. We'd have found a way to ship it to another realm if we'd known. My poor cat looked miserable. Even he wasn't without a heart.

"Fine, take us to it."

Mr. Mittens leaped down and trotted to the path to the waterfall. The spring was about halfway there. We followed.

"Do you know how to take care of a baby unicorn?" Gabe asked.

"Not a clue. Hopefully, Jim has some ideas. Otherwise, I guess we treat it like a horse foal?"

I hoped that was true. Horses ate grass and grain on this planet, but unicorns ate meat. Of course, all mammals on this planet, whether cow or carnivore, drank milk as babies. Maybe the unicorn would be fine on milk. I didn't even know how old "very young" meant.

We found the foal curled up in the grass not far from the carcass of its mother.

It attacked me when I was patrolling, Mr. Mittens said sadly.

The foal was well hidden, and it was easy to see that he hadn't known about it. I used my earth magic and sank the unicorn mare into the earth. The baby was asleep, curled up tight. It was darker than the first unicorn I'd run into, although its mother had been pale gold. The foal was brown, but it might fade to gold when it grew older.

"Why hasn't it set the woods on fire?" I asked. Unicorns could control fire and generally had flames that served as mane, tail, and feathered fetlocks. This one just had hair, like a horse, and only a bump where its horn would be.

I've heard that they don't get their flames until they reach maturity. Same with a full-sized horn.

"Hmmm." The foal was small, but I didn't think I could carry it very far, and I had no way to get it to follow me, if it even would. When it woke up, it would probably frantically search for its mother.

Gabe solved that for me. He scooped the small creature up in his arms and held it, one arm across its chest, the other under its bottom. Its gangly legs hung down. It stirred some and gave a plaintive whinny, but it only struggled a little. The position kept it from getting any purchase to kick or escape.

"It's ill," Gabe said.

Gabe was a supernatural healer, which made him uniquely qualified to know that.

"What's wrong with it?"

His face scrunched up. "I think it's some kind of birth defect, but if I don't heal it, it won't make it very long. It's only a day old."

His gift was very useful if he could tell all of that. I had a few seconds wondering if it would be best to let the little thing die. Its mother was gone, and its race was monstrous. But it was tiny and helpless, and it seemed wrong not to help.

"Can you fix it?"

"I don't know. I can try, but I'm not familiar with its anatomy. I might save it, only to have it develop wrong." He sounded uncertain.

I put my hand on his arm. "I know you, Gabe. You can't stand to see it suffer. Fix it. You can only give it a chance. We'll worry about the rest if it works."

He nodded. I sensed the warmth of his magic more as actual heat that poured from him than as magic. Since I'd reintegrated my full range of elements, I'd been more sensitive to all magic, even magic that wasn't Fae.

The little unicorn struggled a bit more strongly after

Gabe finished. Gabe grunted with the effort of holding the little guy.

"Can you carry him all the way back?" I asked.

"I got it. Let's go."

That sounded like it took a lot of concentration, so I followed Mr. Mittens, and Gabe followed me.

The little unicorn sent out desperate, piercing whinnies, probably calling for its mother, which of course, went unanswered. It broke my heart.

Once we were back, Gabe sat on the porch, the foal in his lap, and I called Jim. The magic that concealed the path to the waterfall interfered with a phone signal.

As usual, Jim listened quietly while I explained the problem. His only response was, "I'll be there soon," and then typically, he hung up without saying goodbye.

I sat next to Gabe. The foal had fallen back asleep, exhausted. I stroked its little face and soft muzzle. "I'm sorry my life is a dumpster fire. We can't even make it out the door without a problem lately."

He chuckled, quietly. "It's not a dumpster fire. You have a pretty good life, I think. I know I like being a part of it."

I leaned into his arm and rubbed his back. "Thank you for not running away as fast as you can."

"Hell, you keep me from ever being bored."

I was rarely bored, so I got it. I was usually too busy keeping things from killing me, so there was that.

Before Jim showed, a baincallan came running up to me across the parking lot. I couldn't remember her name—which wasn't a surprise. I was terrible with names.

"Lady, we've captured one of your vampires. Sorcha said to come quickly."

I looked at Gabe holding the foal, heard the truck coming up the drive—which was probably Jim. Before I could respond, a huge clatter made me jerk, and I stared at the house as Megan yelled, "Stop, you little shit!"

"Go, Brigid. I've got this." Gabe looked at the foal. "Megan can handle that." He tossed his head to point over his shoulder.

I shook my head and stood, as Mr. Mittens strolled after the baincallan.

"Sorry, Gabe, I'll make it up to you," I promised and followed my cat.

Chapter Eighteen

The baincallan must be stronger than even I knew because Sorcha had the vamp's face down in the dirt, her knee in its spine and its arms pulled back. Another baincallan had a spear aimed at its heart.

I frowned because the mass of hair that floated around the vamp seemed familiar. Her voice confirmed it as she shouted, "Get off me!"

It was Bella. I don't know how she'd messed up so badly. I'd have thought her too clever to get caught, especially in the fading light.

I gestured that they should pick her up, which they did effortlessly. Bella was tiny, and apparently didn't weigh much either, particularly when the woman pulling her up was twice her size, and supernaturally strong.

"What are you doing here?" I asked simply.

"What do you think?" she snarled. "I'm spying on you."

"Apparently not very well," I added. "I guess Vic ran out of spare old vamps if he sent you to do his dirty work."

Her face stayed still, trying not to give anything away,

which did the opposite of course. He was out of old vamps. We'd been right.

"You should have died in that explosion." Her face twisted in an ugly snarl, teeth exposed.

I shrugged. "Oh well. You win some, you lose some."

She tried to pull her arms free from the grasp of the two baincallan that held her. They didn't budge. "What are these freaks? They aren't vampires."

"No, they aren't. They are baincallan from Faerie."

"I don't know what that is."

I shrugged again, she didn't deserve more of an explanation.

"Ladies, if you wouldn't mind, we're going to take her back to the house. I think she'd be a lot more pleasant as a human."

Bella spat and hissed like a wet cat. "Human? You can't do that! It's impossible."

I laughed. "You are wrong. Seems my boyfriend has a gift that works just fine on vamps. Once we change you back, I think you might be more willing to help us with the rest of your...what do you call it? Vendetta?" I turned to walk away, and I heard the baincallan dragging Bella along.

About halfway back, she started to beg. "No, please don't. I've been like this for a millennium. I don't know how to be human. I have enemies; they'll kill me. I need to stay strong!" And more of the same. I ignored her. She'd tried to kill me and my friends, and apparently had if my grandfather's report was true—he couldn't lie.

I let her beg and scream and carry on. I had them drag her up onto the porch, while I went in to get Gabe.

"You're back," he said. "Is everything OK?"

"They caught Bella. I think you need to *heal* her."

"Why is she injured?" He looked slightly confused, then realized what I meant. "Oh."

He followed me out. The baincallan kept a firm grip on the vamp as she fought and attempted to shift repeatedly. No matter what she did, she couldn't break free. She looked up at Gabe as he approached her.

"No, no, no!" she screamed and redoubled her efforts.

She actually rocked the two guards, but they braced themselves and held her firm. Finally, she wilted, resigned. Gabe put his hand on her head, and I felt the warmth of his magic stir.

Bella screamed loud and long, then crumpled. I had the women drop her on the deck, which they did. I thanked them and sent them back to their patrol.

Gabe and I stood over Bella, who'd fainted or something. I'm sure it was a big shock to her system to go from ancient vampire to human in seconds. I studied her face, which was shockingly peaceful in her slumber. Gone was the unnatural paleness to her normally olive skin tone. Her cheeks were flushed pink. Her hair was still dark brown with those odd caramel and blonde highlights, but now there was a streak or two of grey as well, and her previously unlined face had natural creases in her forehead and around her mouth, with a few fine crow's feet around her eyes.

As a vampire, I'd have placed her age as mid-twenties, but now? Maybe closer to my age. Of course, she'd been on the planet for much, much longer. Gabe placed a hand on her again to see if she was recovering.

I raised my eyebrow in question.

He shook his head. "Her system is in all kinds of turmoil. Her body is trying to find a balance, but I think her aging is trying to match her true original age. We can only hope it stops soon, or she'll die."

I hadn't really wanted that. If I had, I would have just staked her. I wanted information, and I'd thought that she'd be easier to deal with if she couldn't kill us or drink anyone's blood.

She groaned, and her eyes moved under her lashes.

"Is she waking up?"

Gabe looked down and frowned. "Maybe. The aging has slowed down some."

There were a few more fine lines, but she looked about the same. I wondered if she'd been older when she'd been turned. I knew so little about vampires that I supposed it could be possible. Rather than aging centuries, she was reverting to her initial state.

"It's stopped," he said.

A middle-aged Bella opened her eyes and wept.

Gabe stood and backed away. He was conflicted. As a healer, he had more than his share of compassion, and a crying woman, no matter how foul a person she was, confused his sensibilities.

I reached down and offered her a hand. She looked at me with hate but took my hand, and I pulled her up. "You've killed me," she said.

"You're breathing."

"You know what I mean."

"I really doubt anyone will recognize you. Especially if you cut your hair. It's the only distinctive thing about you now. Well, that and your size, but there are tons of short women out there."

Her hands flew to her face. "No!"

She looked the same, if older, with the corresponding lines and softer skin around the jowls and throat that went with that. She was still pretty. She was slim, and her hair was truly unique. I'd place her close to a human fifty.

"I would have been young forever!" she screeched. "I was powerful, strong. There was only one person in the world I had to answer to!"

I thought for a moment she was going to throw herself at me. So did Gabe, because he took a step forward to protect me. But instead, she buried her face in her hands.

"This is the twenty-first century. You don't have to answer to anyone at all, you know."

"You don't understand."

I looked at her oddly. Did she stay locked in a room when she wasn't trying to destroy me and mine? "I think I do; I've lived in this world since I was born."

"We are only women. Now, I'm back to weak and worthless and needing a man to tell me what to do."

"That's how you were living? I think it's time you stop."

She shrieked again in frustration. She pointed to Gabe. "You only say that because you have a man to take care of you. I can't go back. They'd tear me apart and feast on my blood."

Gruesome thought. I threw Gabe an apologetic look.

"Look, Bella. Let's take you in, get you some food, and we'll talk. Gabe is my partner. We chose one another, but all of this?" I waved my hand around. "Is mine. I bought it, had it fixed up. I own it. Gabe has nothing to do with it. For having lived in this modern world, it's like you never were part of it."

She looked up, bleary-eyed.

Gabe nodded at her. He looked amused and a little disturbed. I wondered how old Bella really was. That was a lot of messed up thinking that had to come from a way different time. Plus, she'd basically lived enslaved to a master vampire for who knew how long. This was going to be a project. I could tell. Me and my great ideas. Next time, I'd stake first. Maybe Mr. Mittens had the right idea.

Chapter Nineteen

I took her in and fed her. Megan sneered at her when we walked past and headed up the stairs. Her face was white, though. I put Bella up in the only room I had left on the third floor. I asked her if she needed anything, and she said no and slammed the door in my face. Typical. At least she was out of the fight for now.

"Are you OK?" I asked Megan when I came down.

"Yeah. Now I can stab her and know she'll die." She shrugged, but looking at her face, I knew it was bravado.

I asked Gabe and Megan about the unicorn and whatever had happened in the house earlier.

"The foal is fine; it's with Jim. He's got it set up on a bottle feeding routine. We'll probably have to help; he'll let us know," Gabe said. That was one thing off my plate for now, anyway.

"What happened in the house?" I asked Megan.

The tight line of her mouth slashed across her face, a sure indication she was miffed. "One of those kitsune brats jumped up on the counter, knocking everything off, and took off with my phone. I wanted to smack it on the nose with a newspaper. But I remembered it was a small child at the last minute."

I tried to hold back a smile. I wanted to smack the whole family on the nose but couldn't, for obvious reasons. Plus, they were annoying, but not more than just mildly troubling. I hadn't thought about my missing keys all day but frowned when I remembered.

"Any sign of my missing keys?"

Megan shook her head. "Do you think one of the brats took them?"

"I don't know. It was either them or the psychic, but I don't know why she'd take them."

Megan frowned. "On those shows where the psychic helps the police, don't they use the victim's personal items?"

I tilted my head in thought. "This whole house is a personal item. Why would she need my keys, and for what?"

"Did you search your rooms for anything else missing?"

A shiver ran down my spine. I hadn't. I was only looking for the keys, and I hadn't bothered with anything else. "No."

Gabe followed me to my room. I had blown our chance to go out to dinner. I hoped he forgave me and that our date later in the week would make up for it. He was too good. He ended up playing second fiddle to my crazy life most of the time. Once inside, he closed the door and pulled me in close. He did well at picking up on my stress levels.

"I'll help you look," he said. But with him there, I forgot to care about my keys.

He sat on the bed, and I followed, straddling his legs and leaning my forehead against his.

"Stay?"

"I'd love too."

I shook my head, and then leaned back down. "I mean move in. We're constantly running back and forth. My life is crazy, and we barely see each other."

He answered by kissing me. Kissing led to more.

When I woke up a couple of hours later, Gabe was gone. He left me a note. *"Early shift tomorrow. Love you. I'll call you after work."*

I cleaned up and searched my bedroom. Other than my wallet, which wasn't missing anything, the only other valuable items I had were Dana's balls, my grandmother's jewelry, and her journals. I opened my dresser drawer. The bags with extra fireballs and the healing balls were still there, as was my ball to contact Faerie. I knew how many healing balls I had, and they were still there. I had no idea how many fireballs, but it appeared to be a full bag. I closed the drawer. I checked my bathroom vanity next, where the jewelry box was. It was all there. I breathed a sigh of relief. Some of those were not only valuable, but sentimental.

Someone knocked on my bedroom door. I opened it, and Megan stood there.

"I heard you moving and banging things that weren't Gabe," she said with a lascivious grin.

"Ha ha, he went home."

"I know. I told him goodnight."

She looked down at the bag in my hands.

Megan's eyes opened wide. "Were some missing?"

"I don't know, it seems full, but I didn't count, and I don't know how many were in there to start."

"If even one of those was taken…"

I nodded. Dana's fireballs packed a big punch followed by magical fire. If someone used one of those in the inn, it would cause major damage. The whole place could go up. I needed a better storage facility or a fireproof safe.

"Remind me to order a fireproof safe," I said and moved over to the bed. I kept the journals under it, mainly because I'd been lazy and hadn't found a permanent place for them. I should put them on the shelves in my drawing room, which had a wall of bookshelves. I knelt down and looked under the bed spread. Nothing but dust bunnies and my missing keys.

I pulled them out and showed Megan.

"They're gone."

"What's gone? The keys are in your hand?"

"The journals."

Megan sat in my reading chair. "What was in them?"

She knew some of what was in them, mainly the spell to summon a certain Fae lord.

My face must have communicated that, because she huffed and said, "What else is in them?"

I shook my head. I'd read them, but other than regular family drama and a few girlish spells, nothing was that interesting. Had I missed something? How did anyone else even know about the books?

"Do you think children would take a bunch of dusty old books?" I asked suddenly.

"Not in a million years."

"I don't think so either." I took a deep breath. "Get your master key and your sword. Something isn't right, and we're going upstairs to see what is going on."

Megan scoffed. "I always have my weapons, since…" She waved a hand.

Since she'd been attacked by a master vampire. I knew that. I nodded.

I pulled on my magic and kept air and ice close. I didn't want to burn down my inn with fire or lightning.

We left my suite, and I locked the door behind us. I still wasn't sure how the psychic had gotten in.

"What's her name?" I asked out of the blue.

"The psychic?"

"Yeah."

"June North."

I nodded. Then I kept thinking "June" in my head because I was terrible with names.

We walked up the stairs to the second floor. Megan's door was the last one on the right and encompassed a turret room along with her bedroom suite. It was nearly identical to mine, other than the paint scheme.

Next to Megan was June, the kleptomaniac psychic. I knocked firmly on the door. No answer.

"Did she leave?" I asked.

Megan shrugged. "I guess she could have on Madison's shift, but I didn't notice her leaving on mine or coming back tonight."

I grasped the master key and held it up to the electronic lock. It flicked green, and I opened the door. The room was dark. The shades had been pulled, and no lights were on. I flicked on the light.

The floors were all wooden, original to the house except where repairs had been made because of the change to the room configurations and a nasty group of witches who'd been looking for my magic before I bought the house. Each room had a rug at the foot of the beds that matched the individual paint schemes. This one had been removed, giving the occupant a decent sized space with which she'd painted a ritual circle. She'd *painted* it on my newly refinished floors. I wanted to hurl lightning bolts.

My hair swirled around my head in anger. Megan rested a calming hand on my shoulder.

"It can be fixed," she said.

I took a deep breath, and my hair fell back down my back. There were candles placed along the circle, and my grandmother's books were open to various pages on the bed.

"What do you think she was trying to do?" I asked.

Megan skirted the circle and looked at the books. She took out her phone and started clicking pics. "Check this out."

I leaned over. The different books, when placed like this, formed a complete ritual map, along with words and instructions. "How did she know how to do this?"

A voice came from the open doorway. "I'm psychic."

Both of us wheeled around in surprise. I felt a moment of guilt for being unannounced in a guest's room, then I remembered she'd stolen from me.

"How dare you take my things from my locked room," I said coldly.

"Who said they are yours?" she answered.

My eyes opened wide in shock, and I started to shake. "Because they belonged to *my* grandmother, and I found them in *my* house."

She shrugged. "They belonged to *my* grandmother."

I frowned. What the hell?

Chapter Twenty

"If my grandmother is your grandmother, that makes you my..."

"Cousin is close enough."

"So why did you steal from me and come here under false pretenses?"

She shrugged. "It's a long story."

I crossed my arms over my chest. "I've got time."

June crossed the room and sat on the comfortable high-backed chair next to the bed. Megan sat on the bed, and I dragged the office chair over from the desk to face June.

She sighed. "Lucy Rose had two children."

I jerked. That wasn't right. My dad had been her only child.

"She found herself pregnant soon after her husband died. She lived alone in this house with her son, and because of the time, she couldn't let anyone know that she was expecting. It was clear that the babe was conceived after her husband's death—a small indiscretion when she'd needed comfort.

"When the child was born, she found a caring, desperate couple to take it, and then made sure that the child had a trust fund to care for it. That baby was my mother, Rose North. Your aunt."

That story wasn't that long. I guess she'd meant she didn't want to tell it.

"And she somehow knew about these?" I waved at the opened books.

"Lucy Rose kept in touch. Grandmother told my mother once she knew that my mother was expecting me. She indicated that when the time came to awaken my powers, she'd leave the ritual in her journals."

"Do you also have Fae elemental power?" I asked.

June frowned. "Fae?" She shook her head. "My mother was a witch."

I froze. I hated witches with a capital H. Witches were bad news. To use their power, they had to keep their inner well full, and most were happy enough to steal that power from others, like me.

I knew that Lucy Rose was half Fae, half witch. But the Fae power seemed to overwhelm the witch parts, at least with me and my grandmother. I didn't know about my dad. I had nothing to tell me what magic he'd favored, if any. But June's mother had been a witch? If June was also a witch, why did she need a ritual to awaken her power? That sounded more like something for a Fae child, like me.

"You are a witch?" I half asked, half demanded.

She shook her head. "I followed the ritual with precise perfection." She stared at my ruined floor. "Nothing changed. I am a psychic. Nothing more."

I relaxed slightly. I'd never ever trust another witch, even if she was a cousin.

Megan had been perusing the open books. "Witch

power is inherent," she said. We'd both learned that the hard way. "This ritual is to unlock latent Fae power."

"Why do you people keep saying Fae? We come from a long line of witches."

I frowned at her. "Lucy Rose didn't tell your mom?"

"Tell her what?"

"Her father was a Fae lord." I waved around at the house. "Fae gold bought this land and built this house."

She shook her head and slumped. "No, no one told me or my mom."

"She must have realized early on that your mom didn't show any Fae power. Maybe she was saving her from a lifetime of disappointment."

"Was your grandfather a witch too?" Megan asked, still reading.

"Yeah, from a local coven. I think he was the husband to the local coven leader."

My head snapped up. They'd been friends—the local coven leader and Lucy Rose. She'd been the one to kill my grandmother. Was it because of the affair? Or only to steal her magic?

Megan looked at me. We had the same thought. I shook my head slightly. We'd keep that to ourselves.

"Maybe that's why your mother only had witch powers," I said instead.

June frowned. "Maybe. My father was human. I guess I've got what I got, and I'm not going to get more."

I seriously doubted it. I would think since the ritual didn't work that there was nothing else to awaken. My powers had to be blocked and stripped as a small child, so either they'd awakened mine early, or they popped up when they wanted to. Who knew? I guess I could time-walk back and ask, but possibly changing my own history made me nervous. That could have ramifications for my present and future.

"I'm sorry I took your books. I thought because I'm from the wrong side of the sheets, you wouldn't be happy to share them with me."

I shook my head. "I love knowing I have some family. I thought I was alone."

June looked abashed. Her cheeks flamed, and she hung her head slightly.

"You are as welcome to the books as I am. How about I have copies made for you?"

She lit up. "You'd do that?"

"Of course!" Then I had another thought. Grandfather would probably like to know he had another great-grand-child in the world. Would that mean that Mr. Mittens would have to split his time between us? I should probably intro-duce him to my new cousin as well. I almost opened my mouth to say something when Megan grabbed my arm.

"We'll take these and get them copied," she said. "We'll leave you alone. Sorry we barged in."

I looked at her strangely, but I trusted her, so I followed her out.

Once we were downstairs, I asked, "What was that for? I was going to introduce her to Grandfather."

"Yeah, but before you do, I want to verify her story. My gut says something else is up. She could have made that whole thing up with facts from these books. I trust her as far as I can throw her."

That gave me another involuntary shudder. I was too trusting. Tell me you're my family? I'd go nuts trying to make it true. I had to trust Megan's gut. It was better than mine.

"You think she's lying?"

"I think you'd have read about your grandmother's indiscretions in her journals. She wasn't shy about things there."

Goosebumps erupted on my arms, and cold fingers ran down my spine. I was a fool. My grandmother had said outrageous things in her books, and she hadn't been shy about recording her other experiments with men in her youth. Something shady was going on. And the woman upstairs? There was a chance she wasn't my cousin.

Chapter Twenty-One

"If she isn't my cousin, why is she doing this?" I asked Megan. I was deeply disturbed. Mainly because I'd been taken advantage of more than once, and I didn't know what she wanted or what she was up to. It didn't make sense she'd be doing this if she wasn't my cousin.

"I don't know, but it has something to do with that ritual." Megan looked devious. I loved that about her. "I took a few pictures. Let's see what we can find out about her and it."

I had the books, so first, I found the pages from Megan's photos, and opened the books to the corresponding ones. I still wondered how she knew what was in the books if she *wasn't* a cousin of mine, but Lucy Rose had witch friends and those witch friends could have known this and passed it to their children. Damn, I hated witches. They'd been the bane of my existence for some time now.

We studied the pages and what the book said. It wasn't much. That wasn't going to stop Megan, though. That was why she had done research for me at my old company. She was tenacious, like a bulldog with a bone.

"I've got this. Stop hovering." She waved me away. I laughed and left.

It'd been a long day. I had chaotic kitsunes and a lying psychic who might be a witch. I had a baby unicorn and a human ex-vampire, not to mention the ongoing issue of the griffinettes that was not being dealt with. I closed my eyes and rolled my head to loosen my neck. I needed to go see Brightfeather. This was something that would bite us if we didn't deal with it. I walked to the kitchen and grabbed a diet Coke from the fridge, then I called my cat and went to wait for him on the back porch. It was mostly dark. I could fit in one more task.

Mr. Mittens came strolling up to me. I don't know where he came from, but he always seemed to appear from the direction I wasn't watching. It was probably a cat thing.

He blinked his large blue eyes at me.

"You ready to check in with Brightfeather?"

He perked up some. He really did enjoy the griffin. *You promised to bring meat for the little ones.*

Crap. I'd forgotten. "What should I grab?"

Hmpf. I'll be back.

I made to stop him, but what was a little while longer? I wondered what he was going to kill for the hatchlings.

I sat on the back steps and scrolled through my phone. I watched a few cat videos. About twenty minutes later, Mr. Mittens showed up at the edge of the woods in his Splintercat form. I walked over to him. I was sure he was trying to avoid notice from any guests. When I got nearer, I saw he had a deer at his feet.

He picked it up when I grew near, and we realm walked to Brightfeather's nest.

"Brightfeather," I called out.

You may enter, Brigid.

"I have Mr. Mittens, and we are bringing meat for the hatchlings," I added.

Please come in.

I went in first, and Mr. Mittens entered with the deer's neck in his mouth, dragging the carcass along between his front legs. He placed it near the entrance.

The hatchlings stirred and started calling out like baby robins for a worm. They must have smelled the fresh meat. Brightfeather snatched the deer in her beak and started tearing off chunks and feeding her brood. We stayed out of the way until their hungry cries died down, and the deer was halfway gone.

The babies watched us, their big eyes engaged but unafraid. Little Brigid, my namesake, cheeped. I looked at Brightfeather for permission, then sank my fingers into her baby fluff, and gave her a good scratch on the head and a belly rub. Her little wings were still just growing stubs, but she wanted a good scratch under them as well.

She remembers you.

I felt strangely moved by that. The baby tried to climb on my lap. I scooped her up and set her in the middle of my folded legs where she demanded more scratching. Mr. Mittens collapsed back down to his Ragdoll form and leaned against me. He reached up and put one enormous paw on the baby's head. She cheeped at him.

I looked at him oddly, but he didn't say anything, just looked for a moment and put his paw down. I guess we were lucky he didn't want to hurt her. Maybe it was his way of communicating.

"Brightfeather, I feel like we need a plan for your in-laws."

She sighed, her breath fluttering through the downy feathers of the chicks.

Indeed. I must tell them about Umber. I should travel to their nest. That will be the best way to avoid them knowing about my children.

I nodded. "We'll take care of them. How much time do you need?"

She stared at the griffinettes. *Two days. I've been avoiding it because I don't want to leave them.*

I took a deep breath. Two days was a long time to babysit. "Tell me what to do."

Feed them. They are warm and comfortable here. They will need to be fed four times a day and kept safe from predators.

I nodded. I couldn't stay in this nest all day. But we could rotate care, I supposed.

I will do it.

I looked at my cat. "You want to take care of the babies?"

I am able, and I can find food. He puffed out his chest. *I will only need help when I leave to hunt.*

Well, that took some pressure off. Unless we had a vampire attack, Mr. Mittens was a very good protector. I wouldn't worry about anything killing the chicks, and I would check in and let him leave to hunt. This could work.

"We'll handle it. When do you wish to leave?"

I will leave in the morning.

I nodded. Mr. Mittens and I left. He followed me into the house, and I made his supper. "You're sure about this?"

Hmpf.

That was his way of calling me an idiot. I'm sure a two-hundred-year-old realm walking cat could do whatever he said he could. I let it go.

Chapter Twenty-Two

I walked into the reception area in time to see Megan chasing a one tailed kitsune kit around. She was muttering under her breath. And from her red face, she was either overheated or blazing mad.

I sent a puff of air magic to stop the kit, and Megan grabbed it by the scruff of its neck. Something was in its mouth, and I realized it had taken her phone again. I stifled a laugh.

"Drop it, you little beast."

The fox's eyes flicked to me, pleading, but I folded my arms.

It opened its mouth, and the phone dropped into Megan's hands.

"Shift," I said sternly.

The fox shifted into the girl that had been making our lives miserable. Megan set her down.

"Where are your parents?" I asked firmly.

She shrugged but kept her eyes down.

"Are they in your room?"

That was enough. She started to cry. I rolled my eyes for Megan's benefit. She tucked her phone in her pocket and went over to the desk. I saw her dial the room.

"Mrs. Nishiyama?"

There must have been a reply.

"Your daughter is downstairs unaccompanied. Please come and get her immediately."

Megan remained calm and firm. I was impressed. I wanted to shake the entire family. She hung up, and I picked up the little girl and set her down on the reception desk.

"We don't take things that aren't ours," I said to her.

She rubbed her little eyes and smeared snot across her cheek with her sleeve.

"I was going to give it back."

"I'm sure you were. But if you don't take anything, you don't have to worry about it." I grabbed the tissues on the desk and wiped her face.

"You also need to be with your parents, OK?"

She nodded and stopped crying. I could hear a door shut upstairs, mostly because it was more of a door slam.

"Your momma is on her way down. Be good."

Mrs. Nishiyama stormed down the stairs. She glared at us but didn't say anything. She scooped up her daughter and headed back up. I still didn't understand why she thought we should be watching her children, but it annoyed me to no end.

Once she was out of earshot, Megan said, "The nerve of that woman."

I agreed.

"Do you want to get some dinner? Chef Jack made his famous six cheese chicken fettuccine."

"Good lord, yes, I'm in."

We headed to the kitchen. Both trying to walk through the door at the same time.

"How does this happen to us all the time?" Megan griped as we bounced through, both of us almost falling.

"Because we're two doofuses."

Jack looked up at us and grinned. "I left you two plates warming in the oven."

I started to salivate. I pulled both warm plates out and set one in front of each of us. Chef Jack placed a basket of warm and toasty garlic bread in front of us, and we tucked in.

"This is so good!" Megan mumbled with her mouth full.

I jabbed her with my elbow.

"Well, it is!" she said.

"Has our new guest been down?" I asked. I'd basically left Bella half the day, which wasn't the smartest plan, but I didn't have time to watch her.

"She ate an hour ago. I assume she went back to her room," Chef Jack said.

This time, Megan answered with an empty mouth. "Yeah, she went back up."

"Did she say anything to you?"

Megan shook her head. "I'd like her too. I owe her a punch in the teeth, but I think she knows she's walking on thin ice with me."

I felt some tension ease. Bella had no reason to call any of her companions. She was too vulnerable, and I doubted she had anywhere to go. This was her safest bet.

When we were done, the craziness of the day hit me, and I felt exhausted. "I'm going to bed," I said to Megan, and she nodded.

"Me too. It's been a long day."

We finished up, cleaned up our dishes, and left. Mr. Mittens was waiting in the middle of the bed for me. "Are you tired too?"

I should rest. I have two busy days ahead of me, he answered.

"Are you OK with this? Have you done much babysitting?" I looked at him intently, gauging his response.

Hmpf. I watched you as a baby.

That surprised me. "Really? My parents left me with you?"

Often. They knew I wouldn't let anything harm you.

I left him to groom and went and cleaned up for bed. Mr. Mittens was snuggled into his fluffy blue cat bed on top of my bed when I came out. Thankfully, my bed was king sized, because he took more than his share of the room. I climbed in, and it felt like I fell asleep before my head hit the pillow.

Chapter Twenty-Three

If disaster struck in the middle of the night, I didn't know about it. I slept hard, and only Megan waking me up worked. I must have slept straight through my alarm.

"Dana is here for my lesson," she said. "We'll practice in the parking lot, but she wants you to have a lesson at the waterfall when I'm done."

I groaned and sat up. "I'm helping Mr. Mittens with the babies today. Brightfeather is going to go speak to her in-laws, *finally*."

"You tell Dana. I don't like to give her bad news."

I wrinkled my nose. I didn't either. Dana was one of those people who would stomp on you, and the only thing she'd feel bad about was the mess she had to clean off her shoe. "Ugh. I'll help after the lesson, I guess."

"Smart."

"Has Brightfeather been by yet?"

Megan shook her head. "Not yet. I think you have some time."

Megan left because you did *not* keep Dana waiting, and I

took a quick shower and dressed for a lesson and for feeding three hungry griffin babies.

Madison was at the front desk. "Hey Mads," I said. "Any shenanigans this morning?"

"It's been remarkably quiet. Probably because everyone left on day trips today, even the kitsunes."

"Thank heavens. They've been running us ragged."

She snorted. "Tell me about it."

"Oh, Jim mentioned that the kids went over to the fishing pond and tried to convince him I sent them there. Did they say anything to you?"

"No. But the parents try way too hard to pawn the little brats off on anyone that isn't moving fast enough to get away."

I frowned. I *knew* they were deliberately trying to get free babysitting.

"Don't give in. We do not offer childcare services."

"Don't worry."

I nodded and went to grab some breakfast. The two maids were already there eating, so I greeted them.

In the kitchen, I could hear metal against metal and figured it was Dana and Megan practicing in the parking lot. I grabbed a cream cheese bagel and headed out to watch.

They already had an audience. Goch sat in the far corner, his broken horn and scarred cheek making me cringe. One of the baincallan watched from the tree line, her eyes sweeping the area with precision before returning to the training session. Mr. Mittens watched from the porch railing.

"I'd thought you'd be at the nest?" I asked him, curiously.

It seems our favorite griffin is not ready to leave her hatchlings so soon, he said drolly.

"What happened?"

She told me she needs another day. They are only two days old, and she can't bear to leave them.

"I hope her in-laws give us another day." I searched the skies for an imminent landing; they appeared clear.

Hmpf, was his reply.

The swords clanged together again, and I finally looked at the lesson going on. Dana was tall and mostly green, not that her color affected her sword work. She just had a lot of reach on Megan, who was human and of average height.

Dana was closer in size to the baincallan women. Only they shifted to something that looked human or, more realistically, high Fae. Dana could not pass for human or Fae. She looked more like her kelpie half, only twisted into humanoid form rather than equine. She had two arms and two legs, but instead of feet, she had hooves. She had two large eyes that faced forward like a humanoid, but they had no white sclera, and if you stared into their black depths long enough, you could see her distinctive horizontal rectangular pupil. She had the pointed ears of the Fae, but they were set on top of her head and were a mix between her Fae and kelpie ancestry. She didn't have a true muzzle, but her face was long, with large nostrils and heavy lips. When she did open her mouth, like her kelpie side, she had viciously sharp teeth, more like a shark than a horse. Kelpies, like unicorns, were meat eaters. And finally, although she wore Fae robes and lived like a high Fae, you could see the twitch of her tail under her silky garments.

She lifted her sword arm and positioned her sword horizontally over her head. Megan copied her. Then she showed Megan a foot position. They swept through other forms.

Megan looked good; she seemed to have a knack for physical combat. I watched them go through several forms again, and then they went back to slow motion sparring, the swords ringing as they struck each other.

I gave my cat a few ear scritches, then walked down the stairs, skirting Megan and Dana, to check on Goch. He was watching intently.

"How are you feeling?" I asked.

I'm feeling better. My horn doesn't hurt anymore, and the scratches aren't as bad unless I bump them. He looked over at Mr. Mittens. *Do you think he'll talk to me now?* he asked, hopefully.

I didn't know, but it was something I could fix at least. I looked at my cat and sent a pinpoint message to him. "It's time to make up with Goch. He's sad. Get over here and tell him you'll take him hunting."

Mr. Mittens' eyes bored into mine from across the parking lot. *I'm still angry.*

"I don't care."

Hmpf.

But he jumped down and strolled slowly our way.

I'm sorry, Mr. Mittens. I'll listen next time, Goch chattered as soon as the cat joined me.

Mr. Mittens sat next to my leg and stared daggers at the dragon. *Yes, you will, or I won't take you again. I'm trying to keep you from getting yourself killed.*

The dragon looked miserable, but he promised.

Fine, I forgive you, Mr. Mittens said.

You had to give my cat credit. He could slap a kid into line with words or literal slaps. I should set him to work on the kitsune problem.

When can we go hunting again? Goch asked eagerly, his previous depression thrown off and his usually sunny disposition shining back through.

The weekend. I have duties here until then. You'll have to hunt in the woods, my cat told him.

That only dampened him back down slightly.

I can't wait! Goch looked like he was going to jump up and spin on his tail, but I reminded him where we were, and he crouched back down to watch.

I looked back at Megan. Her hair was damp, and her shirt was soaked. She was dragging. Finally, Dana called it. Great. Now I was up. Megan gave her a salute and headed to the house. Dana found my eyes and flicked her head to the waterfall trail. I groaned.

"Be good," I said to the cat and the dragon and headed that way. Dana's sword had disappeared, and I assumed she also stored her weapons in her magic balls. She already disappeared up the trail, the masking spell hiding her from me until I crossed the invisible threshold of my grandmother's old spell.

She was waiting for me at the spring, about halfway to the waterfall. I looked at her curiously.

"Are you practicing your magic daily?"

I looked at her oddly. I did, usually because I just had to use it to survive, but Mr. Mittens made sure I did.

"Yes, of course."

"I do not need to observe. I just wanted to talk to you privately."

That surprised me, and my eyebrows climb up my forehead.

She handed me a set of three magic balls. Unlike the others, they weren't a set color or the texture and size of a marble. The color pattern in each one moved and swirled. They felt squishy to the touch, like a stress ball, although I knew enough about Dana's balls not to attempt to squish them. I'd probably be exploded into atoms if I did so.

They were about the size of a super ball, so larger than normal.

I looked up, a question in my eyes.

"The red ball is the one you requested of me—a shield for the house. Place it where you want the entrance to be and stomp on it hard while whispering the names of those that you allow entrance to. If you wish to disengage it, stand in the spot where you activated it and say, 'Brigid.'"

That should be easy to remember. "Is it reusable?"

She looked annoyed, which she usually did, but she answered, "It has three uses. Be sure before you activate it. This was difficult to make, and it takes time to build." She looked away for a moment. "I'm afraid a strong magic user might be able to penetrate it. I was unable to test it to my satisfaction."

I felt a momentary irritation that she'd sent me untested products, but she was doing this as a favor, and it was better than the current nothing I had now. I nodded. "And the others?"

"The blue is a pain inhibitor."

I'd intended to ask her to make one for Goch, but I hadn't gotten around to it yet. My face must have shown my confusion.

"Megan requested this for your dragon. Since it would have to ingest several medical balls for pain, this was more efficient. It's for an area rather than an individual. Activate it by casting in on the ground, and however many creatures you place within its boundary will be pain free."

I had one strange ball left, a green one. I held it up.

"The green is a weapon."

I instinctively held it at arm's length.

She ignored my reaction. "If you throw it at your

enemies, it will portal them into the dungeon of your grandfather's keep."

Then she added with a grin. "I need some new subjects for my experiments."

I shuddered. She could have all the witches and vamps she wanted, in my opinion.

"It'll transport ten if they are close enough together. Unfortunately, it is a one use spell."

Awesome. At least it wouldn't go boom and take out the house.

"Let's see if I've got this. Red is a house shield, Blue is pain relief, and green is the dungeon?"

"Correct. I must return, but please try to make yourself more than adequate."

"I appreci..." She flashed out before I could thank her cleverly.

I turned to head back.

Chapter Twenty-Four

When I entered the kitchen, Bella was sitting and eating breakfast. Chef Jack was keeping a sharp eye on the ex-vamp. While I watched, Megan walked in and sneered at the vamp. She turned around to leave.

"Wait," I said, and motioned for her to sit.

She wrinkled her nose in disgust and took a chair as far away from Bella as she could.

Bella sniffed and tasted everything before she put it fully in her mouth to chew, which had to be driving our chef batty, no pun intended.

She looked up at me when the weight of my stare grew too heavy. "What?"

I shrugged. "I've just never seen anyone eat like that before."

"I haven't eaten solid food for a thousand years. I remember it wasn't that pleasant of an experience, so I'm being cautious."

"You didn't like to eat?"

"I don't remember. I'm sure I liked to have a full belly. I just don't remember that many foods being available."

They probably hadn't been unless you were wealthy.

"I am trying to reacquaint my palate with the smells, textures, and tastes of solid food," she snapped.

"Didn't you eat real food as a vampire?" I knew Vic Constantine could eat; I'd had lunch with him once.

"No, I did not enjoy anything but blood."

I chose a chair, pulled it out from under the table, and sat. "Do you have somewhere to go?" I asked her. She hadn't really spoken to me since I had Gabe "heal" her.

She glared up at me. "Not anymore, thanks to you."

I ignored her. I figured my obligation to her for changing her had been met. "Do you have access to money?"

She shrugged. "I did. Everything belongs to the Vendetta. If I accessed my funds, they would know. Then..." She swiped her thumb over her neck. I got the picture.

That could be tricky. But they knew she was in town or had been yesterday.

"Could you pull out a stack of cash and disappear before the vamps awakened for the day? I mean, they don't know you aren't your nasty vampiric self."

She'd been the enforcer for her Vendetta. Surely, that meant she knew their security measures and could avoid them.

She stared at me for a moment but didn't say anything.

I seriously bet she had money hidden somewhere. She was too sly. If she'd really been alive a thousand years or more, she probably had several stashes.

"Your best bet is to go somewhere you know they won't

look, change your name, and live as a human. I bet no one will even look for you."

She gave a disgusted snort but went back to sniffing and tasting. I just wanted her gone. I felt guilty enough to give her a twenty-four-hour respite, but that was over.

"I can arrange for transport to the airport if you wish."

"No. I'd have to arrange for a new ID to do that. I need a car."

"If I find you a car, will you leave?"

She shrugged. "Yes."

"Fine."

"You need to answer some questions first, then we'll make sure you get out of here with a vehicle."

"What?" She said nastily.

"How many old vamps does Vic still have?"

"I can't tell you."

"You can go stay in a Fae dungeon if you want."

Megan gave a snort laugh.

She glared at me. "I don't know, a few."

"Three, then?" I smirked. I knew he had to be low on old vamps.

She shrugged but wouldn't elaborate.

"Why did he blow up the yacht? That seems like an expensive mistake."

"What's it to you?"

"I'm curious."

"It needed work, and he stole it from a rival. A win-win."

"Why does he want us gone?"

She sniffed and looked at me. "He prefers to be the top predator."

"I'm not a predator."

"Aren't you? Don't you control the werewolves, and didn't you kill the witches?"

I thought for a moment—that thought disturbed me. I didn't control the werewolves; we were friends. As for the witches, well, they started it.

"Why are you such a bitch?" Megan added into the silence.

Bella smiled one of her wide grins designed to show all of her sharp teeth. It didn't have the same effect now.

I held up a hand to stop Megan before a brawl broke out. She was still hot under the collar, and I was afraid blood would be drawn now that the scales between them were tilted in Megan's favor.

I stood, and Megan followed me out. Chef Jack would keep Bella from doing anything stupid.

"You're going to buy her a car?" Megan asked dubiously.

"I'm not gonna buy her a Lamborghini. I'll find her something that runs and send her on her way. I'm sure there are plenty of vehicles being sold on the internet right now."

Megan shrugged. "True."

I didn't have time for this, but I was sure I could find a car quickly and have Bella gone by the end of the day. At least it would be one thing checked off my list. I headed to my computer in my private drawing room.

A woman was sitting on the stairs sobbing. I looked over at Madison, who was at the front desk. She shrugged helplessly.

I couldn't see her face, but from the hair that was hanging down, I guessed it was the human mate to the angel.

I couldn't remember her name, so I whispered a question to Madison, knowing the woman wouldn't hear me.

"Brooke Ellison," Madison whispered back. I had to give her credit for not rolling her eyes. This was twice I'd had to ask.

I sat down on the stairs next to the sobbing woman.

"Are you OK?" I asked softly.

She sniffed and shook her head. I grew slightly alarmed. I was probably suffering a little PTSD myself from the deaths of my first guests, so I took a deep breath and tried to focus.

"What happened?"

I looked at Madison for direction, but she appeared as baffled as I did.

The woman shook her head but didn't answer.

"Do you want me to get your husband?"

"He's on a fishing trip."

"Oh." I thought for a moment. "Why don't you come into the drawing room? It's private, and you can talk or not. I'm a good listener."

She stuttered out, "OK," and let me lead her into the drawing room, which I unlocked and led her to sit on the plush sofa. I sat next to her for a minute to see if she wanted the company.

"My mom called."

I made a noncommittal noise and waited.

"My dad has cancer. It's not anything new, but she called to tell me to get home now. This is the end." She started sobbing again.

I was alarmed. Why was she still here? "Do you need help getting back home?"

"I don't know what to do. They aren't speaking to my husband. We came here for a break from the family drama. I need to go, but…"

I took a deep breath. I was about to sandwich myself

into another family's drama, but in my heart, there was only one right path, and I couldn't believe her husband would disagree.

"Look, I don't know you or your family, but if you don't see your dad before he passes, you'll regret it for the rest of your life."

"You really think so?"

"I really do."

"OK."

The poor, meek little thing just needed someone to push her to make a decision. "Do you know what guide your husband is fishing with?"

She nodded.

"Let's call and get your husband back. You go pack up. OK?"

"Y-yes. Thank you."

She pushed back her hair and rubbed the tears out of her eyes. She gave me a tentative smile and headed out the door, looking at her phone. I heard her give the message to whomever answered and start back up the stairs. Things were never easy when you worked with the public.

I logged on to my computer and started looking for a car so I could get rid of my ex-vampire nemesis.

Thirty minutes later and I had four decent possibilities. I printed off the information and went up to Megan's room to give them to her. I didn't have time to go out and check on the vehicles, but I hoped Megan did.

I knocked.

"It's open," Megan said. It wasn't really open, she usually kept it locked, but Megan knew it was me. I scanned my master card and opened the door.

Megan was in her bathrobe, hair up in a towel. She'd obviously just gotten out of the shower.

"What's up?"

"I found some cars that might work for Bella. I was hoping you could go look at them?"

She folded her arms. "Why do you think I'd help that conniving mini ho?"

"Because you want her gone ASAP?" I said and fluttered my eyelashes at her.

"You suck. I do want her gone."

"So?"

"Fine. I'll go." She sighed, used the towel to squeeze out as much water from her hair as she could, and shooed me out.

"I'll leave these here!" I said and dropped them on her bed.

Then I headed out. One task checked off the list. Now, to go and convince a griffin to take care of her issues before they bit us all.

I didn't bother calling my cat. He apparently had a secret life where he trained mortals and did his own thing. Maybe I was a little miffed at him, but when I walked to Brightfeather's nest, he was already there. Of course he was.

He had brought another deer, so that was good. Maybe it would help us convince her to go. She couldn't delay. I doubted they'd give us another day before they showed up and started looking around for their son.

She still looked tired, and I sensed her deep stress.

I know what you are going to say, Brigid, she said.

"You know you have to do this. Otherwise, they'll come here."

She sighed. *I know. It's just so hard to leave my babies. They need me.*

"Of course they do; you're their mother. They will

always need you. However, they won't have you if you don't do this. You know your in-laws will come back, and they will search the woods for their son. You'd do the same for little Brightstorm."

She gazed down at his downy head. *I'd do anything.*

"Good, go do it. We'll keep them safe and fed and warm."

Mr. Mittens added his assurances and tore off a chunk of meat to give to little Brigid.

I don't know what to say. She hung her head in misery.

"Tell them the truth. He died protecting you and his friends."

What if they want to come back here and see his grave?

"Then take them to the grave. It's far enough away that they shouldn't find your nest."

What if…

I interrupted her. "You'll 'what if' us all to death. Just do it. We'll deal with the fallout later. They deserve to know."

She gave a very uncharacteristic moan. *You are correct. I need to get it over with. I'm just afraid for them…* She looked down at the helpless little fuzz covered griffinettes.

I understood. But if they came here, I didn't know how we'd keep them secret. This was the only path I saw forward where we could keep them hidden until they were old enough to make their own decisions.

She heaved herself out of the nest. Little cheeps followed as she exited. She kept looking back. I knew she'd left to find food for them, so they had to know she'd be back. I followed her out. She looked rough. Her feathers weren't clean and many were out of place. Her tiredness could be mistaken for grief, and I was sure she felt that as well.

I'll be as fast as I can, she said. *Thank you.*

"Don't worry, everything will be fine," I replied. I really hoped it would be. If she kept the griffins off our backs, and the vamps stayed away, we had nothing really to worry about except for a family of annoying kitsunes.

She stretched. Wings unfurled, she shook, and her ruffled feathers fell mostly into place. She beat her wings a few times, then using her powerful lion haunches, she launched herself and spread her powerful wings. I watched her rise slowly above the trees, the wind of her powerful wingbeats swirling my hair and forest litter around me. She shifted into her grey eagle form, then she rocketed off and disappeared from view.

I walked back into the nest. Mr. Mittens was dutifully shoving meat chunks into the hungry beaks. "Are you OK by yourself?" I asked.

Of course. I suggest you have one of your new guards accompany you while I'm busy, he said. I wanted to laugh at my killer cat playing nursemaid, but he was so serious and solemn I didn't do it.

"Do you want me to come back later and spell you?"

That would be acceptable. I'll need to bring back more meat. They eat a lot for such tiny things, he remarked.

I looked at them intently. "They've grown, you know."

Hmpf.

"They'll be too big for this nest soon."

Once they've outgrown it, they'll be able to fly and hunt for themselves, he said smugly, like he was the only one who knew how it worked.

"I suppose so." I scratched little Brigid's fuzzy head, and she cheeped at me, her eyes soft and gooey as they looked on me with love. I smiled at her. "Be good for uncle, little ones."

Uncle? Mr. Mittens asked.

"They have to call you something once they can speak."

His chest puffed out. He looked smug. *That would be acceptable.* He looked at the little creatures. *You will call me Uncle Xrsrphn*, he announced proudly.

"I think it'll be a while before they can handle that moniker, Mr. Mittens."

They are very smart.

There was the proud uncle. "Yes, they are. See you later." I stepped out and walked back home.

Chapter Twenty-Five

I stepped into the parking lot in time to see three tiny children disappearing up the trail to the waterfall. At least they weren't in fox form. As usual, not a single parent could be seen. They shouldn't be able to see the trail, let alone walk on it. It repelled most people and only... I don't know what I was thinking. They were heading up the trail that my cat wouldn't let me walk alone. If it was too dangerous for a woman with thirteen magical Fae elements, it was too dangerous for three little children.

"Dammit," I said out loud and ran after them. "Stop!" I bellowed as I headed up the trail. The two oldest looked at me and giggled. They scattered.

I pulled out my phone and texted Madison. "All kitsune children are on the path to the waterfall. Get their parents now!" and put it in my back pocket. I wasn't a runner, but I did know that things that were being chased tended to run faster to get away. So, I slowed down. The toddler, who had to be only two or three, was only in its diaper. It was April, but it wasn't that warm. I was wearing a long-sleeved shirt and jeans, and if I slowed down, I could feel the chill. The baby had to be freezing. Sister and brother had either shifted or just disappeared in the brush. I scooped up the baby, who was just about to cry.

I didn't know what to do. Should I take the child back to the house and then look for the others? Would they be safe if I did? There were wild animals and supernatural creatures in these woods. I encouraged all guests to stay on a marked path and explore with a partner, but this path wasn't on the list. I only allowed the path from the fishing pond and back and one next to the house. I didn't need any more dead guests.

I balanced the baby on my hip. I'd have to take it back. "I'm coming right back; you need to be here when I return," I said to the woods. Some rustling and a stick snapping were the only responses.

I turned and headed back down the trail.

When I reached the front desk, I had somewhat of a plan for the kids. "Madison, does the pack have daycare?"

She cocked her head at me. "I don't know. That's a good question. We do have a few families with small children... I'll text Noah."

She pulled out her phone and started texting. The kitsune parents obviously needed a break from their kids. Maybe I could arrange a complete break for everyone for the rest of their time here. I still didn't know why they even brought the kids, but maybe they didn't have reliable childcare at home.

"Can I leave this one with you? The other children scattered, and they aren't in a safe patch of woods."

Madison eyed the dirty, half-naked toddler warily. "I'm not good with kids."

"Join the crowd. Hopefully, your brother has a solution

JILLEEN DOLBEARE

for all of us. I can't take two more days of these little wild beasts. Mr. Mittens is on griffinsitting duty so he can't chase them, I've got vampires breathing down my neck, and a pair of griffin royals that will want to tear my head off when they find out it's my fault their son is dead." I took a deep breath.

Madison held out her arms for the toddler. I thanked her and headed back to the trail, stepping onto it in time for both children to come screaming down the trail right at me.

"Monster!" they yelled.

I scanned the trail and the trees beyond them. I didn't see anything, but there was a good chance a monster was in here somewhere. Mr. Mittens was constantly killing the things. The kids ran up to me and clung to my legs. I frowned. Just then, a monster came strolling down the trail. The kids were wrapped so tight around my legs I couldn't move, not even to take the required step to realm walk. I looked at the horror approaching. It was huge and covered in dark fur. It was vaguely humanoid, but instead of a human shaped head, it had the head of a bull complete with huge horns.

The kids were shaking, and their little faces were buried in my legs. I couldn't do anything. I reached down and held on to them as I looked into the eyes of the beast.

I wasn't trying to frighten them, a warm voice said in my head. *They were alone in the woods. I was trying to keep them safe.*

"You won't hurt them?" I said, making sure I heard correctly.

No! I was just out for a walk. I'm staying here.

Damn! This was my minotaur, and I hadn't even met him or my other guests yet, three days into their stay. I was a terrible hostess.

"It's OK, children, run back to the house. Chef Jack will give you a cookie."

They looked at me tentatively, but the idea of a cookie was clear in their eyes, and finally won out over their fear. They ran down the trail yelling "Cookie!"

I hurriedly texted Jack to let him know what he was in for before I remembered it wouldn't go through until I cleared the spell to the trail.

Then I addressed my minotaur guest. "I'm Brigid, the owner. I'm so sorry I haven't been by to welcome you to the Secret Haven Inn."

He gave me a solemn bow. *Charmed.*

That was formal. If I hadn't known where he was from, I'd wonder if he came from the Fae court. I gave a little curtsy. All those previous queen classes had to be worth something.

"How do you like my woods?"

They are charming indeed. A nice change from my usual haunts.

"I'm happy that you are enjoying them. I'm very pleased to meet you, but I need to go wrangle the children. Please, excuse me."

He nodded, and I turned and hurried after the kids. Hopefully, Madison had an answer for me when I returned.

The kids had a cookie in each hand. So, Chef Jack gave them one even without the warning. It was hard to resist their cute faces, no matter how bratty they were. I didn't know about filling them full of sugar, not when the parents weren't doing their part, but they were quiet and occupied for a minute. I hurried through and checked in with Madison.

"Hear anything from Noah?"

She looked up. "Yes, we do have a daycare for the wolves. Actually, for the next two weeks, they are doing a summer day camp for all the children. I asked and Noah has given permission for the kits to participate. You just need to get permission from the parents, and they'll need a ride to and from."

I felt a big old wave of relief. We could give everyone a big break from the wild children.

"I forwarded the forms to your email."

"Thanks, Madison. Cross your fingers they'll go for it!"

She held up both hands with crossed fingers. I unlocked my drawing room door to print the papers. I froze. June North, my fake cousin, was pulling books off my shelves.

"What are you doing?"

She whirled. I'd caught her red-handed. "I..."

She reached down and plucked a trashy novel from a shelf. "I needed a reading book, and the books weren't out yet..."

I had a small portable bookcase for a "take a book, leave a book" sort of deal. It usually sat outside the door of my drawing room, but it was still inside. The maids must have mopped this morning, moved it, and forgot it.

"The door was locked," I said simply.

"Oh, it was? I walked right in."

I knew it was locked, and she'd locked herself in as well because I'd had to unlock it to enter.

She smiled, clutched her book, and hurried out. Somehow, she was getting into my locked rooms, and she was looking for something. Something specific. I wondered what she was after. For now, I had a task. I sat at my desk and pulled up my email.

Once I had the copies to enroll the kids in summer camp, I locked the door behind me and hurried up to the Nishiyama's door. I knocked.

This time Mr. Nishiyama opened the door, but only a

crack. "We have the do not disturb sign hanging on the door."

"I know, and I'm sorry to bother you. The children are running around again and it's not safe to leave them unsupervised." Before he could say anything, I rushed on. "I have a solution."

He squinted at me, and the door opened a centimeter more.

I thrust the paper permission forms into the crack. "The local werewolf pack is hosting a summer day camp for children two through twelve. I thought maybe the kids would like to go for the next two days."

"Hold on." He shut the door. I waited, wondering what he was doing. Hopefully, talking to his wife.

I waited ten minutes, and finally I just turned to leave. I was halfway to the stairs when he opened the door. "Yes, we'll enroll the kids."

I hurried back to the door. "The only stipulation is you need to drop them off and pick them up."

"That's fine." He pushed the papers back at me through the tiny crack in the door. Boy, were they weird.

I grabbed the papers. They were all filled out. They must seriously want to get rid of the kids—that was some Olympic level form filling.

"I'll send these in."

He shut the door. Crap, I still needed to return the kids.

I grinned at Madison and waved the papers around. "We won't have to worry about them after today!"

She lifted her arms in a victory salute. "Yes!"

I looked around. "Where's the baby?"

"He's in the kitchen with the other two."

I flinched. Poor Chef Jack. He didn't sign up to babysit. I hurried down the hall. I burst into the kitchen, expecting to see Chef Jack packing up his knives. Instead, there was a six-hundred-pound tiger playing horsey for three small children. He was galloping around the table, and they were whooping and urging him on.

I stopped and stared. Chef Jack rounded the corner and came to a cartoon stop. The kids slid off over his head and giggled. The tiger disappeared into the laundry room, to dress, I assumed. Sure enough, he came out a few minutes later.

"Thanks for watching them," I said.

He looked abashed. "We had fun."

"I'm sorry they were dumped on you. I've managed to get them enrolled in a camp for their last two days, so they won't be in your hair."

"It's really no bother," he said.

I rallied the kids and pushed them out the door. I loaded them in the elevator and took them up to the third floor, where I left them with their dad—who was not happy to be getting them back. It was odd to me they were so blasé about the children. Weren't they worried? Oh well, I'd found someone who'd care for the next two days. I started down the stairs in time to hear Megan walk in.

I hurried down. Megan and Bella were snarking at each other, so I hurried to interrupt.

"Did you find a car?"

"I sure did, and it's perfect," Megan said.

"It's hideous. I wouldn't be caught dead in it!" Bella added.

I frowned at Megan. It would be like her to find the most repellent beast out there to pay Bella back, not that I cared as long as it ran long enough to take her away forever.

I quirked an eyebrow at Megan.

"It's in the parking lot."

They both followed me out. Parked in the middle of the parking lot was a grape-colored PT Cruiser. But the fun didn't end there. It had hot pink and yellow flames licking up the sides, spinner rims, a lighted undercarriage, and dark tinted windows.

"I had a G-wagon." Bella sighed. "It was the best."

"You've been upgraded," Megan said with a grin. "It has all the bells and whistles that they offered in 2005. It's a classic, you know; they don't make these beauts anymore!" She clapped a hand down on the flaming hood.

I had an inner chuckle. I knew Megan thought PT Cruisers were the ugliest cars ever made. She probably looked for one specifically. I wouldn't have gone for the flames, but I thought the cars were kind of cute.

Megan opened all four doors. The interior was custom hot pink leather. It looked like the whole thing had been washed with Pepto-Bismol, or Barbie was going to peek out with a cheeky wave and an invitation to her Malibu beach home.

"It's really pink," I said with a lilt to my voice. I was trying to be positive for Bella.

"I detest pink," Bella said.

I could see that. I bet her favorite color was black or crimson. She probably thought charcoal was a bright, happy color.

I leaned in further and checked out the entire interior. The inside looked newly redone, which other than the pink had to appeal. It even smelled like new leather. Something this old should smell a little moldy after existing in the temperate rainforest for its lifetime.

"It runs, and was recently completely overhauled and a new interior put in to match, you know, the flames," Megan added. "It was an excellent price as well. A steal really…"

Megan's shit-eating grin wasn't helping her sell the car's appeal to Bella. Bella still looked like she'd sucked on a lemon.

"Anyway, here are your keys! Enjoy life on the road!" She dumped the keys in Bella's hand and gave a little finger wave. "Toodles." She added a shooing motion as though Bella was an annoying fly.

Bella frowned at the keys, then at the car.

"No one will ever suspect that it's yours," I added hopefully.

Bella appeared to chew on that, staring at the car with her head cocked to the side. "You're right. It's brilliant. No one will ever think that I would even *ride* in that monstrosity."

She stared at me a moment, and I had the distinct feeling she was going to thank me before she remembered I'd stolen her immortality and power. She gave me a snort and tucked herself into the car. I imagined anything of importance was in her pockets, since she hadn't had anything visible with her when we'd captured her. It didn't matter. My guilty conscience was assuaged. I had done all I could and treated her with the respect due any human being. I waved as she turned around and faced down the drive. She gave me a last look, a half nod, and she was gone.

One enemy removed. I knew I had a minimum of one more. I didn't know what he had left to fight with, but I was proud I'd removed one knight from the chessboard, and I didn't have to feed her to my cat. Win-win.

Chapter Twenty-Six

I thought about the minotaur and the baby unicorn, and although I had a lot of things going on, I knew I had to go and at least check in on my other guests. Jim would never complain, and he'd figure out issues on his own, but it wasn't fair to just leave everything on his shoulders. I went to call my cat and stopped myself. He was busy. If anything happened, I'd deal with it. I was capable. Instead, I grabbed Megan.

"Wanna meet a real kelpie?" I asked.

"Dana is real enough, but sure!"

One thing about Megan, she was game for anything. "Would you rather walk across or drive around?"

She thought. "I think I could use the exercise."

I was hoping she'd say drive, but I could probably use the exercise as well. "Fine."

We walked, and I filled her in on everything that had happened, starting with Brightfeather, Mr. Mittens, and the hatchlings, the minotaur, the summer camp, and June North.

"I feel like we've been two ships passing in the night lately," she said.

"Yeah, it feels like that. I also didn't realize how much I relied on my cat. I keep wanting to call him and have to stop myself."

"He's a lot more capable than a regular housecat, for sure."

I snorted. "You could say that."

We laughed. I glimpsed one of the baincallan in the woods and relaxed a bit. Even without my cat, I was safe and watched over. We cleared the trees soon after and let ourselves in the gate at the back pasture. A few animals grazed quietly, enjoying the sun, a rare occurrence this time of the year.

Once through the fields, we looked for Jim. He was always busy. I spotted his side-by-side near the main barn where the guests were staying, and we headed that direction.

He was just inside, sitting on a stool, and he was giving the unicorn foal a bottle. The little thing was attacking it hungrily.

"You should give him a name," Jim said without looking up. I'd hardly even thought about the little thing since I'd left it with him. I felt a twinge of guilt.

I looked at Megan. "Any ideas?"

"Hell-beast?"

"It's just a baby,"

"True." She sighed. "Maybe it'll be nature vs. nurture. We'll nurture it so it won't turn into a big dick."

I chuckled. "We should probably start with a really positive name."

"I guess that means Satan is out."

"Usually."

"Lucifer?"

"Megan, seriously."

"Fine…Angel? Brownie? Sweet Baby Demon?"

I laughed. "I think I'll come up with something by myself."

"Probably better. The last unicorn ruined my favorite stretchy pants. I'm not in a good place to come up with sweet names."

"I've been calling him Milk Dud," Jim added. "He stole one from my pocket. It was funny watching him try to chew it up."

That was cute, but Milk Dud was a terrible name. I'd have to think about it. "How's he doing?"

Jim shrugged. "He's drinking the milk, he'll eat a little grain, but he doesn't have those sharp teeth for eating hay. I'm thinking of adding a little hamburger to his diet in a couple of weeks. He hasn't lost any weight, so I think the horse milk replacement is working."

That was the most I'd heard Jim talk. "Do you need help with him?"

"We're doing fine."

"How are the guests?"

"They're also doing fine."

I nodded. "Anything I need to do?"

He shook his head. He was either scarily competent or just didn't want anyone in his space. Maybe a little of both.

"We'll get out of your hair then."

Megan and I wandered down the long corridor between stalls. They were all closed, so that's all we did. We exited through the door on the opposite end of the one we'd entered and ran into the minotaur.

"Good day!" I said, brightly.

Megan stared. I bumped her with my elbow. "Hi!" she added, belatedly.

It is lovely running into you again, the minotaur said with one of his courtly bows.

"Are you having a nice stay?" I asked.

I am, indeed.

"Well, if you need anything, don't hesitate to ask," I said.

He thanked me and wandered off. We headed towards the barracks building to see what the Whelan's had accomplished so far.

I knocked because there were probably one or two bain-callan off duty. I was surprised when Sorcha opened the door.

"Brigid, how are you?" she asked warmly.

"I'm good, just checking on the building progress."

She ushered me in. The men were currently working—Noah, Luke, and a few of their workers I didn't know. I wondered if they were also werewolves, but I didn't ask.

The end of the building was already walled off and the rough plumbing in for a shower room and toilets. It looked like they were flying through the work, although I knew there had to be drying time for the tile they were putting in.

It was also loud and must be hard for those that were off duty to rest. Sorcha and one other woman were perched in front of the TV. I guess they'd figured out how to find things to watch. I pulled out my phone and ordered a few large bean bags. That would up the comfort level.

Sorcha and the others hadn't seen any other vampires since they'd brought in Bella, and I was hoping the danger had passed now that Vic Constantine's army of old vampires had been so severely reduced. Maybe the danger was over.

Splintered Secret

After that, we stopped at the fishing pond. I wanted to see the kelpie, and the pond was the best place to do so.

Megan stayed behind me, a little nervous. Frankly, I was nervous too, but having water magic was my best defense— I hoped.

We stopped next to the little boat dock where a rowboat was moored for guests. I didn't see the kelpie, so I walked out to the end and peered into the water. A little frothy wave erupted from the center and started moving towards me. My heart clenched for a moment, and my breath caught. I focused on my water magic, just in case.

The kelpie erupted from the water and galloped towards us over the surface. It was similar to a horse, if horses were greenish and had frothy white manes like sea foam.

It whinnied and tossed its head when it stopped in front of us.

Have you come to play with me? It asked.

I shivered involuntarily. "No, sorry. I'm Brigid, the owner of the Secret Haven Inn. I'm sorry that I'm late welcoming you, but I'm here to do so now."

The horse placed a hoof on the dock and heaved itself up. Once it was there, it shifted into a green-skinned man. Unlike Dana, who was a mix of kelpie and Fae, this man had the perfect form of a high Fae, outside of his skin color.

"I'm enjoying the facilities immensely," he said and gave a little courtly bow. I had to say the creatures visiting were amazingly courteous, unlike the visitors to the big house.

"And the pond, is it satisfactory?"

"Yes, I've enjoyed having it to myself. Although it is a little lonely. I think next time I'll bring a friend."

I beamed. Next time? Yes. Maybe the Inn would be a success.

"We won't bother you, just wanted to check in," I said.

He waved us away, shifted, and galloped back to the pond, where he sank beneath the surface.

"That was cool," Megan said.

I nodded.

"The only guest I haven't met yet is the wyvern."

"Is that like a dragon, but only two legs?" she asked.

"Yes, why?"

"Well, I saw something like that flying with Goch earlier."

"Oh." I wondered if I should panic or be grateful my teen dragon was helping out. Until I learned something different, I guess gratitude should be it. "Let's go."

"Yeah, I'm hungry. Think dinner is ready?"

"I hope so. I need to eat and go give Mr. Mittens a break."

"When is Brightfeather going to be back?"

"She said tomorrow. I hope all is well."

"Me too!"

Chapter Twenty-Seven

I wasn't expecting Brightfeather very early. However, I heard her calling me right after I ate breakfast the next day.

I ran out to the parking lot just as she spiraled down to land.

"How did it go?" I asked, panting.

I am afraid, she said. *They know something is up. They'll be coming to see the grave and probably search your land. I'm sorry.*

"You have nothing to be sorry about. I made a promise to protect you and your babies. Let me think, and I'll be out to check on you soon. We'll come up with something."

You are a good friend, Brigid. Thank you. She gave me one sad look, launched herself back into the sky, and headed towards her nest.

Damn. One more thing, and it was a doozy. How we handled this could lead to a war with the griffins. I didn't think I'd survive a war with the vampires *and* the griffins. I needed my cat. He might have suggestions—or somewhere he thought we could hide the babies.

I sat on the porch steps. I don't know how long I was

there, but it was long enough that Mr. Mittens strode out of the trees. I'd felt the magic pulse that let me know someone had realm walked, so I supposed that's how he was so quick.

He strode up to me, gave me a body length rub on my leg with a head butt, then jumped up on the railing.

"Did it go well?"

Hmpf. Of course. Everyone is alive and fed. I'm a cat of my word, he said testily.

"I didn't doubt it. We have a problem."

His blue eyes focused intently on me. *More vampires?*

"No, they might be easier at this point. Brightfeather fears that her royal in-laws will be back, and they'll conduct a search of the land. We need a way to hide her chicks."

Did Dana not give you a new protection ball?

I started. I'd thrown the balls she'd given me into my dresser drawer with the others. Then, because we'd caught Bella and removed her from the vampire side, I'd promptly forgotten about them.

"It would keep them out, but they'd still be seen."

Hmpf. You forget that you are full of magic. You are nearly unlimited in this place. Place your shield and make the nest invisible. I've seen you do this before. He jumped down and laid on my lap with his feet in the air. *I have an itch under my right arm.* He stretched it out so I wouldn't miss the spot, and I gave him a good scratch.

I sighed. I could do it if there wasn't a wind. In fact, the shield might assist in holding the illusion. I cocked my head; I wasn't sure what it would do. Should I ask Dana? Would she smite me if I kept bugging her? Worse, would she stop making me magical trinkets? I'd missed her earlier during Megan's sword lesson, and I didn't think I could wait until she came tomorrow. That meant a trip to Faerie.

I continued working my fingers through his long fur, finding all the itchy places as he wiggled around to aim my fingers. "Would you consider doing me another favor, oh great and marvelous cat master?" I asked sappily.

He turned his head so he could open one eye and stare at me from his upside-down position.

Dare I ask? I don't have to watch those annoying kitsune kits because that is a step too far.

"No more babysitting. I sent them to summer camp."

Indeed? He rolled over to his belly and stomped around in my lap before he plopped back down.

"They were driving everyone crazy. Now they can bother the werewolves for two days."

What is the favor?

I took a deep breath. "Walk to Faerie and deliver a message to Dana? Please?"

You do realize that the only person she despises more than you is me? Do you not?

"Really? I hadn't noticed." Mainly because he made himself small or scarce when Dana was around now that I thought about it.

I could speak to your grandfather instead if you have a magical need?

My cat was cracking me up. He faced down unicorns, killed creatures twice his size, and he was afraid of Dana. I guess that was a great measure of how scary and capable she was. Even though I had more magic and more elements, I was fully aware that I wouldn't stand a chance against her. Not with her portable magic balls anywhere near her.

I'm not proud of myself, but it amused me, so I asked, "Are you afraid?"

Hmpf. He licked one white mitted paw. *I'll go, what is your question?*

"I just need clarification on the shield spell. Would it hold my shadow magic in place within or would it dissipate as it usually does in the air?"

He repeated it back. Made me give him a thorough ear scritch, then got back on his feet. *I'll require an extra bowl of cream for this.*

I gave him one more pat on the head. "You deserve all the cream. Thank you."

He jumped down on the parking lot and took a few steps. I felt the pulse of magic as he realm walked to Faerie.

That answer—depending on what it was—would give us a little wiggle room. The only other option was moving the entire griffin family to another realm, but that would end with permanent exile for my friend and wouldn't help me avoid war with the griffins. We needed a real, permanent solution. And I didn't know enough about griffin society to come up with one. I'd at least let Brightfeather know what options I could offer. She was the one that had to make the decision.

I walked to the nest.

"Brightfeather?" I said as I approached the entrance.

Come in, Brigid.

I did. The little ones were playing, snapping at each other with their tiny beaks, and tumbling around the area as they chased each other.

Brigid was the smallest, and had the weakest beak, but she made up for it with sheer savagery, pinning her larger brother and tweaking his tail.

Brightfeather watched with love in her eyes and a touch of sadness. *I know they'll take them from me, and I'll have nothing.*

"No. There are options. Be positive." I explained my choices—stay and hide the hatchlings, flee to another realm, or try to find a compromise with the royals.

"I'm terrified they won't hear reason if I tell them about the children," she said.

"We wouldn't let that be an option. We'll keep them hidden until they reached a workable compromise."

She hung her head, overwhelmed. *I want to stay and raise my griffins here.* She looked away. *I don't see a path forward where that happens. We'll either be forced back to the court or flee from this realm forever.*

I nodded. I understood. She had to give up her home or her children. I knew which she'd choose, but it didn't make it easier.

"I'll do whatever you wish."

Thank you, Brigid, you are a true friend. I'll think on the choices you've given me.

I nodded and walked back to the house.

Mr. Mittens hadn't returned yet. I wondered if he'd failed to find Dana, or if she was tormenting him. The question shouldn't have taken much time.

I shrugged. I didn't know how much time we'd have before the griffin king and queen came back, but I had things to do until then. Mainly find out what June North wanted and why she was lying about it.

I strolled boldly into the house.

Chapter Twenty-Eight

I met Megan in her room. I'd had her researching June, and I wondered if she'd found any dirt yet. I knocked and slipped in.

Megan was at the desk, pounding words into the keyboard.

"Any luck?" I asked.

"I was having zero luck until I discovered that June North is not her name."

"Really?"

"Yup." Megan plucked a piece of red licorice from the tub of them she kept on her desk and put it in her mouth. "Look at this." She pointed to the screen.

"What am I looking at?"

"You need glasses," she said.

I huffed.

"It says her real name is Amber Bergman."

My blood went cold. I choked out a repeated, "Bergman?"

"Yeah, why? Do you know her?"

I shook my head. I didn't know her, but I knew the name. "Bergman was Sofia's maiden name. Amber Bergman is her little sister."

I sat down on the bed.

"Sheee-it." Megan's eyes were wide.

"She has to be a witch. She's been lying."

"What is she looking for, then? You have all your magic, and she must know that."

"Maybe a link to Faerie for fill-ups? It could be something else entirely, but I can't have her searching this house. I need her out."

"I'll refund her money and send her packing," Megan said with a determined scowl.

"Maybe I should just confront her. Ask her what she wants."

"Has that worked in the past?" Megan asked incredulously.

"No, but neither has doing things the way I've been doing them. At least this will be a change."

"Ok, whatever."

I opened my mouth to argue my point, but the phone rang. I answered it.

"Hi, Madison."

"You have a delivery at the front desk," she said.

"Thanks, I'll be right down."

"I've gotta go. If you think of a better idea, I'll listen," I said.

She waved me off, already absorbed in her computer.

I walked down the stairs. There was a gigantic bouquet of flowers waiting. It was magnificent. I wondered who they were from. Gabe would bring me flowers, but he didn't have them delivered. I think he enjoyed watching my face light up with the pleasure of receiving flowers and other silly gifts like our walkies.

Madison shrugged when I looked at her with a question in my eyes. There was a card, so I plucked it up and opened it.

"Thanks for the advice. We made it in time. Yours, the Ellisons."

I must have murmured *Ellison* in confusion because Madison supplied. "Angel human couple."

Madison was growing accustomed to my blank mind when it came to names.

"Thanks."

That small gesture really sent a warm feeling through my heart. I'd done a small thing encouraging her to go, but it made a difference. I picked up the bouquet and placed it on the decorative table leading into the reception area. It filled the space with color and the gentle scent of flowers.

I was turning around to go to my office when a strong pain lanced through my stomach. I doubled over just as a loud crack like thunder rang through the air and left the smell of ozone behind. Clutching my belly, I stumped to the elevator. The noise had come from the second floor, and Megan was up there. I punched the two. When the elevator door slid open, I stood staring at the wreckage of the room next to Megan's. The door was split in half, lying on the floor, smoking. Megan was standing there, staring at it.

"What happened?" I asked.

"I don't know, I came out here when the door…"

I moved to get in front of her and check out the damage. "Was June in there?"

"I don't know. Madison has the front."

I leaned over the balcony. "Madison?"

"Yeah, I can hear you. What happened?"

"I don't know. Did June North leave, or was she in her room?"

"I haven't seen her today. She must still be in her room."

I had a very bad feeling. At least the sudden pain in my guts was fading. I could stand up straight again. Megan followed me as I skirted the wreckage of the door to peer inside the room.

There was a body lying half on the bed. I gasped and ran inside. She was face down. Her hair spread around her. Hair that had gone completely white. Icy tendrils ran down my spine, and my heart seized. Together, Megan and I flipped her over. It was June or Amber or whatever her name was, but she'd aged fifty years. Under her was another of my grandmother's books. One I hadn't looked at or noticed before.

It was clear that to work whatever spell she'd found, she'd used up her witch's well and drained her life-force with the last of her power. The stupid fool.

Megan felt her neck for a pulse. "She's alive."

I pulled out my phone and called Gabe. He answered on the third ring. "Brigid! How are you, gorgeous?"

I would have let my heart melt at the greeting, but I couldn't. "I have a witch in my inn, and she's almost killed herself. Can you come?"

His voice went from warm to clinical. "Give me ten minutes, and I'll be on my way."

"Thank you!"

We hung up. I stuck a piece of paper from the floor in the book so I could look at what she'd done later. Then Megan and I pulled her fully up on the bed and covered her. Megan stayed while I went to wait for Gabe.

True to his word, Gabe strode through the door right when he'd said he would.

"She's upstairs."

He followed me up the stairs to June's room.

Megan was sitting next to the bed. "She's still breathing."

"How old is she?" Gabe asked and started checking her vitals.

I looked at Megan. "Umm, thirty-nine."

The woman on the bed would pass for her nineties. Before this, I'd have placed her age in her mid-thirties. She must have expended a ton of magic to age so fast.

Gabe placed his hands on her head. I felt the warmth I associated with his magic. He kept his hands there for longer than a minute and then dropped them, frowning.

"Her well won't fill." He looked confused. "It's like it's been blocked."

Megan grabbed the book we'd found and flipped it to the page we assumed she'd been casting the spell from.

Megan stared at it for a long time, finally looking up at me with horror on her face.

"The spell...it's to block *magic*."

"Magic?" I asked, confused. I'd still felt Gabe's attempt to heal her.

"Yes, it's to bind Fae magic." She tossed down the book and started searching the room.

"What are you doing?" I asked.

"The second part is to splinter the magic into parts. This is what your grandmother did to you as a baby! I'm looking for artifacts."

My heart pounded in my chest, and I too began to search. Nothing. She hadn't completed the spell; she hadn't had enough juice. I breathed a sigh of relief.

Just then, Mr. Mittens came strolling in the room. He stared at me. I looked at Megan.

"He says he's been calling to you, but you won't answer."

I looked down at my cat in horror. My magic was gone.

Chapter Twenty-Nine

I shook my hands as though that would activate my power. It didn't work. I felt the world sliding sideways, and then it stopped as Gabe reached out and caught me. He sat me in the chair where Megan had been.

"It's gone," I said helplessly. Then everything else hit me. "I can't help Brightfeather or fight the vampires." I could feel the panic start. I stared into his eyes and saw his love and compassion.

"She didn't finish the spell," Megan tried to reassure me. "It can be reversed."

I felt a little hope awaken. "How?"

"Well, the hardest thing will be finding a witch."

"We need a witch?" Despair filled me again. A witch with the strength to do this kind of spell would be as corrupt as the ones I'd just fought. I shook my head. "Impossible."

She grabbed the book and started searching through its pages. "Look, your grandmother was no more witch than you, and she did this. We could get away with a strong Fae magic user—probably."

Mr. Mittens looked on, his large blue eyes blinking as he took it all in. I looked at him, desperate to hear his thoughts. He jumped up in my lap and tried to comfort me. His large housecat body was shaking with anger.

"I can't even ask you what Dana said." I smoothed his fur, absently petting him, trying to soothe both of us.

He meowed. *Meowed!* It broke my heart. The tears dripped down and wet his fur.

"I guess we need to make a trip to Faerie," I said out loud, my mind racing. I could send Mr. Mittens back, but it would be better to go. Only...I didn't have magic. I drooped. "Dammit. I can't realm walk."

Mr. Mittens stared at Megan.

"He says he can go."

I patted him again. "I know you'd do anything for me. Thank you, but I should go. There is more power there." I thought. "Maybe if you ask..."

A triumphant trumpeting erupted from the back of the house. Goch. I wondered what he'd done. I looked around the room.

"She's stable. Go see what's wrong with your dragon, and I'll stay with her," Gabe said. He knew instinctively I needed a distraction fast, or I would lose it.

I nodded my gratitude, and Megan, Mr. Mittens, and I trotted back down the stairs and out the back. Goch was standing triumphantly in the parking lot, next to a bright green wyvern.

Megan translated, "He says, 'Brigid! I did it!'"

I was very grateful I'd made Megan that charm when she first came to live here.

"What did you do, Goch?" I said. The distraction working, I pushed down my worries about my magic and focused on the dragon—more than a little concerned.

"He says he taught his new friend how to realm walk." He was bouncing up and down slightly in his excitement. I felt my heart warm a little. He was a good kid.

"Why don't you introduce us?" I asked.

"He said it's his new wyvern friend, Dram." Goch smiled a toothy dragon smile, which luckily, I took as happiness, otherwise it would be a bit scary looking at those huge sharp teeth.

"It was very lovely of you to teach your friend a new skill."

"He's gonna show him lots of new realms to hunt in." I threw her a grateful smile for her translating skills.

"You are a good friend, Goch."

I froze. I had a wildly absurd thought. Mr. Mittens couldn't take people with him when he realm walked, but the dragon was a huge creature. If we...*No*. I'd told Megan we don't ride sentient creatures. But, Brightfeather had carried me before. Maybe I could bend the rules?

"Goch, have you ever walked to Faerie?"

"He says, 'Yes. Mr. Mittens took him there to hunt wild cow things. He added that they were delicious,'" Megan translated.

I looked at Megan and Mr. Mittens, then addressed Goch again. "Do you think you could take us to Faerie?"

Goch blinked.

To his credit, he did think about it for a few moments.

He looked somber. He'd sensed this was important.

"Yup," Megan translated.

"Thank you, Goch." Inside I was jumping up and down. I wanted to leap on his back and leave now. I closed my eyes and pulled myself together. There was stuff that had to be done first. I took a deep breath and said calmly,

"We need to prepare, why don't you take your friend back, and meet us here this afternoon?"

"He said 'OK.'"

Goch and Dram sprang up and with a few wingbeats were gone from view.

Megan was ready to jump up and down. "I'm going to be a dragonrider!"

I laughed—my mood immediately improved. "We aren't fighting Thread. Just traveling to Faerie, same as usual."

"Only on dragonback, duh!"

"Yeah. I guess so." I turned back to the house. "We need to get everything ready for the spell, and we need to find something that will keep us from falling off Goch. Any suggestions?"

"Oh yes. I've been preparing for this day." Megan rubbed her hands together with glee.

I gave her a double take. "You've been preparing to ride Goch? Even after I said 'we don't ride sentient creatures?'"

"Yeah, of course. He's a dragon, I'm a dragonrider. It's a match made in heaven."

I rolled my eyes. I should have known.

"Do you have something good? To hold us on, I mean?"

"I made a riding harness. Just like on Pern."

"You did. You?" I said, incredulously. Megan took to crafts like a duck took to cement—not at all.

"Well, I had help." She pouted.

"From whom? Mr. Mittens?"

"What? No, that's dumb; he doesn't have thumbs."

Mr. Mittens hissed at her.

"You are great at everything, but in your cat forms you don't have thumbs, it wasn't an insult," she said to him.

He turned his back on her.

"So, who helped?" I asked impatiently.

"I special ordered it. I even measured Goch."

I sputtered. "You what?"

"He thought it was funny."

I sighed. The teen dragon wasn't the only wild cannon in this bunch.

"So, did it arrive?"

"Yeah, although I thought nylon was tougher than leather, so yeah. And it can be easily modified for two with a simple carabiner."

"OK, that's handled then. Do you have the requisite carabiners?"

She nodded.

"What do we need for the ritual?"

She shrugged. "Nothing big, just candles and herbs and chanting and crap."

"So, what do we need to bring?"

"I'll make a list; I need to recheck the book."

"OK, I guess we'll meet Goch here later. Let's go see what we need to do and hope my grandfather isn't busy."

"Should you call him on your magic ball thing?"

"No. He might show up, and I don't want to bother him when we are going to Faerie. Once my powers are back, we can time walk back here without any issues."

"Right. We do have a house full of guests."

My anxiety was ramping up at that thought. If we weren't successful, there was no guarantee, unless my grandfather was feeling generous, that we could time walk back to this time. And I'd be basically leaving my guests, a dying witch, and the crazy Kitsune clan to my staff, which wasn't cool.

We dispersed, and I ran back upstairs to talk to Gabe.

Chapter Thirty

I'd almost forgotten Brightfeather. Since I only realm walked to her nest, I didn't know if I could find it by regular walking.

"Mr. Mittens, can you explain everything to Brightfeather and let her know that we'll try to be back only seconds from when we leave? She deserves to know what happened and that I'm trying to get it fixed. I don't want her to worry about her babies."

He nodded since I couldn't hear him. Then he took a step and walked. I still felt the pulse of magic, but I couldn't touch mine. It wasn't gone, only I couldn't bring it to bear.

Gabe was examining June again when I entered her room.

He looked up at me when I entered. He shook his head. "She's the same."

"We are going to go to Faerie," I said with a sigh. "I don't know what else to do to get my magic back. Do you want to come?" I added hopefully.

He looked back at the witch. "I would love to go

anywhere with you and see Faerie, but it will have to wait. I need to stay here and monitor her. Plus, I'm on call, and that means I should stay in this realm."

"We plan to time walk back to the time we leave."

He smiled. "We both know that plans aren't necessarily reality."

I nodded. "Yeah, I know. I just want you with me, always."

He stood and walked over to me. I sank into him, and he pulled me in close. "I am."

We stood that way for a few minutes. Then the witch on the bed stirred, and Gabe went back over and laid his hands on her head again.

"She's the same," he said when he dropped his hands. "I don't think she's going to wake anytime soon."

"We'll try to hurry," I said. "Maybe Dana has something that will help her, or I can use a healing ball."

"I don't think it will matter," Gabe said soberly. "If the block isn't removed, and her well can't be refilled, there is nothing to heal, and no way to save her. Even if I refill her well, she may have aged herself too much to recover."

"All of this for revenge."

"Or to steal your power."

I hadn't thought of that. Sofia had tried to steal it from me directly. I guess this was safer. Block me, divest me from my elements, and then take them. I'd be helpless to save myself unlike before.

"Yeah, I guess both."

"Go. We'll handle it here. Madison is great. She can handle the inn, and I've got this."

"Thanks, Gabe. I'm so sorry to dump this on you."

"You didn't. I volunteered."

He pulled me in for a kiss. I breathed in his scent,

clean and welcoming, and my heartbeat slowed as his arms tightened around me. I felt like the world could go away when I was with him, even my crazy world. When he released me, the world came back, and I turned away so he couldn't see my face. He'd been so loving and generous to me, and I'd repaid him with kidnappings, evil witches, and a vampire war. I don't know what he saw in me.

I hurriedly put together a small bag. I'd been meaning to deliver some items, gifts, for my grandfather and Dana, but hadn't done it yet. Then I went to see if Megan needed me to find anything for the ritual.

"No. What I couldn't find here, your fake cousin had in her stuff. I'm good."

"Do you have your harness?"

She lifted a large duffle bag. "Right here."

"Once Mr. Mittens is back and Goch shows, we're ready."

"I need some flying leathers," Megan said randomly.

"You didn't already order some?" I remarked rather snarkily.

"I thought about it."

"We're realm walking, not going Between. Goch doesn't even have to leave the ground."

She scoffed. "We're flying. End of story. Plus, if it makes you feel better, he only knows how to do it from the air."

"You're making that up."

She shrugged.

I shook my head. I wasn't going to fight her. She could live her dream. I just hoped that while she was encouraging Goch to fly with us, she remembered we were over forty and would probably be terribly sore after the whiplash and stress of takeoffs and landings.

Mr. Mittens appeared, the pulse of his realm walking magic warning me.

He looked at Megan.

"He says that Brightfeather wishes you luck, but she is worried."

I nodded. Of course she was. This affected her the most. If her royal pain in the ass in-laws showed up while I was gone or powerless, I wouldn't be able to help her at all.

"He says he'll meet us in Faerie."

I looked at him. "It'll be OK."

He nodded, and with a pulse of magic, he disappeared.

The wind from Goch's approach warned us that it was time. He landed gently in the parking lot. I watched, because I was worried about the physics of humans being launched by powerful dragon legs and wings and what it would do to our bodies. I thought we'd be alright on the landings.

Megan hurried over and set her large duffle bag down, then she unraveled what looked like a mile of black nylon strapping. It looked like she was about to load a military cargo ship.

She laid out the harness. "OK, Goch, lay your neck down right here." She pointed, and the dragon obediently laid down, stretched, and did whatever she told him. It took a while and didn't look like it would be fun to do more than once.

Finally, he'd been strapped and fastened until it looked like he wore a mesh clubbing t-shirt. But his wings were free, and it looked secure.

"How does it feel?" Megan asked.

Goch trotted around in a circle and flapped his wings.

I couldn't hear his answer, but Megan remembered to translate for me.

"He says, 'It's fine, it isn't restrictive, and he can barely feel it!'" She pumped her fist.

"So how does it hold on to us?" I asked.

She answered by handing me a harness.

I looked at it blankly.

"Just watch." She took hers and showed me where it went and how to step into it. Once she had hers on, and it was obvious she'd practiced, she helped me. Soon we were wearing what looked a little like a parachute harness, with straps between our legs, over our shoulders, chest, and waists. "When we get on, this clips to Goch's harness." She showed me the straps with carabiners to clip on.

I took a deep breath. I wasn't that fond of heights, and I had no desire to ride a dragon. It'd been bad enough riding on Brightfeather, and she had feathers to hold on to. My hands would be free, but I'd feel unsafe no matter what. Looking at the contraption he was wrapped up in, he probably couldn't drop us if he wanted to.

"OK. I guess I'm ready." I swung my bag over my arm and shoulder. "How do we get on?"

"Goch, you ready?" Megan asked.

I needed to pay more attention. They'd even practiced behind my back. Megan had probably read the entire *Dragonriders of Pern* series to the dragon. I wouldn't put it past her.

Goch crouched down low and extended his front leg. Megan grabbed onto a strap on the harness, took two steps up his leg and swung onto his back in between a few ridges. With a sigh, I copied her. A little less gracefully—she was in much better shape than me since starting weapons practice.

Once we were clipped on, Megan turned to me and said, "Goch and I think that if we lay as flat as we can against his back, it will reduce the strain from take-off." She laid down and grasped the harness on both sides. I copied her. I was far enough back that I could lie down without my head being on her butt. I grasped the harness like Megan.

She shouted, "We're ready!"

I felt Goch's powerful muscles bunch and with a bone jarring leap, we were airborne.

Chapter Thirty-One

The take-off was immensely jarring, but laying down did alleviate the strain on our necks and backs. Once we were aloft, it was pretty smooth. The rhythmic pumping of Goch's wings was similar to galloping horseback, and when he glided, it was serene. I didn't feel unsafe at all. I even thought I could unclip the harness and I wouldn't move.

Then, Goch banked.

I felt my body shift slightly, and I panicked a little, until the harness caught me, and I knew I was secure. My heart pounded in my chest, and the sweat started pouring off my head. I wiped a hand over my forehead to keep it from dripping into my eyes. Goch circled the parking lot about twenty feet above the trees. Megan raised her fist, the signal to me that he was going to realm walk, and then we were in Faerie.

Hopefully, Mr. Mittens had warned my grandfather, because I'm sure a dragon appearing over his keep was a troubling sight. I could see my grandfather's Fae guards as they noticed the dragon, and their faces did seem surprised. However, no weapons were trained on us.

We circled a few times until my grandfather appeared on the battlements. He had men clear a space on the roof, and once that was done, Goch spiraled in and set down gently on the roof. Mr. Mittens was there to greet us with Grandfather.

"I see you've learned to make an entrance," Grandfather said as we unclipped and slid down Goch's extended arm.

"Had to. Did Mr. Mittens fill you in?"

"He did."

I gestured up at Goch, who appeared very proud of himself. "This is Goch, one of my friends." Goch's large head swung around.

"Goch, this is my great grandfather, Lugh."

Goch's luminous golden eyes blinked once, and I realized he was conversing with my grandfather.

Then, harness still intact, he sprang from the roof. The wind from his wings threw my hair around and battered us all.

"Your grandfather sent him to hunt among his herds," Megan whispered to me.

"I appreciate your concern and care for my friend," I said to my grandfather.

He waved a dismissive hand. "It is the least I can do." He grinned at me. "Now, let's go see this ritual and get your magic unblocked."

I closed my eyes briefly in gratitude, warmth filling me as the comfort of knowing someone capable was about to fix everything washed through me. It was a feeling I hadn't had since my parents died. A safety net. Freedom from a problem I didn't have to solve or worry about because others had my back.

We followed my grandfather as he led us down the steps to Dana's lab. I was nervous. I relied on Dana a lot, and someday she was going to demand a favor in return, or flat out refuse to help. I just hoped today wasn't that day.

We entered her lab. When Dana saw my grandfather, she stood from her desk and bowed. I rolled my eyes. I'd told him months ago that she was in love with him, and he needed to be honest with her. I guess he hadn't done anything yet. Her eyes still gleamed when she looked at him.

Since Megan had arranged everything, and Dana liked her better, I stood back and let Megan explain the situation.

When she was done, Dana looked at me. "You couldn't have done this when I was in your realm?"

I'd kind of worried she'd feel like this, but it wasn't my fault.

"It would have been more convenient for all of us," I responded with a shrug.

Grandfather waited with us while Dana perused the spell. I was lucky she was proficient in English, probably because my grandfather was and frequently went between realms.

She looked up at me and then at Grandfather. "This is a Fae binding ritual."

He nodded. "Yes, it must be the one I gave Niamh to bind Lucy Rose's power when she was small."

That sent a wave of relief through me. If it was a known spell here and used Fae magic, surely they could reverse it.

"It's been modified."

My grandfather frowned, and so did I. That wasn't good.

"In what way?" he asked.

"I'm not sure. I think it's modified to allow a magic user without Fae magic to complete it." She scanned through some more and slammed the book shut. "No matter. The usual unbinding should work."

OK. Not much longer, and the ability to use my power would be returned. I just needed to let the dread go.

Other than the one ridiculous spell I'd used to summon my great-grandfather the first time, I'd never really done spells. I'd used my power—direct elemental power—but I didn't feel advanced enough to try spells. Maybe someday. So, it seemed odd to see Dana set up for a spell. I mean, I guess she did it all the time; she made portable magic, and that seemed like something that would require spells rather than raw power.

She set me in a chair. Unlike the witch's spell, which had included painting my floor with symbols, Dana did none of that. I looked at Megan, who shrugged and dropped the bag of ritual items she'd brought. Maybe witches needed the extra boost from the ritual that powerful Dana didn't in the land of free magic.

She checked the spell one more time, muttering something under her breath. Then she snapped her freaky, too-long fingers.

"That's it," she said.

"You mean, I'm fixed?" I asked incredulously. That was seriously underwhelming.

"Yes."

I looked at Megan, she looked at me. Grandfather leaned against a table. Mr. Mittens had gone looking for some cream, apparently cream on Faerie was superior to cream on earth.

"Well, magic something," Megan said while I sat frozen.

"Yeah, yeah, I should test it." I thought. What was simple? Flame was easy and came to me without much effort—being one of my first elements.

I held out my hand and willed a flame flower to grow. A spark fluttered in my palm, then erupted with huge spitting flames. It grazed the ceiling, which was probably twenty feet up there. "Oops." I closed my hand, and the flames stopped. The ceiling had a small scorch. It didn't look like I was the first one to set it aflame, scorches looked common up there, but I still looked at Dana in trepidation.

"It worked," I announced unnecessarily.

Dana just gave me a dirty look. She was confident it worked just fine. "I taught you better control than that."

I cringed a little. She had. But I'd just powered through, not thinking that what she had done was complex enough to release the block on my power. Boy, I should never doubt Dana.

"Do you think when you removed the block from it, it would remove the block from the witch that cast it?" I asked.

Dana blinked. "The witch that did this blocked herself as well?"

"Yes."

She gave a horsey snort. "The fool. No. I do not know, nor do I care."

Why would she care? I only cared because the woman was a guest, and I didn't need another police investigation— especially with the vampires controlling them. That woman had tried to steal my magic. I thought that was behind me. I had to find all my grandparents' books, journals, tomes, grimoires—whatever form they took—and make sure no one but me would ever see them again.

I grabbed my bag and heaved it up onto one of Dana's tables. I dug around in it until I found the item I had made for her.

I pulled it out. A gleaming new cell phone.

I handed it to her. "You are always making such wonderful things to help me; I thought maybe you'd enjoy this."

She flipped it over and looked at it blankly.

I showed her mine and indicated the button to turn it on. She copied me, and it blazed to life. She almost dropped it.

"There aren't satellites and service on Faerie, of course." I don't know why I bothered to explain she didn't understand those things. "But we have magic. I worked hard to enchant one of these for you and for Grandfather. Now, you call each other anywhere in any realm—and me, of course. Also, you can view videos and make your own pictures and videos of anything you wish."

I walked her through the things she could do on the newly mixed electronic magic device. Magic powered it, now, and a magical connection now linked four phones together—mine, Megan's, Dana's, and Grandfather's, which I had yet to give to him.

Dana appeared fascinated. I wondered if I'd come back to all of Faerie suddenly having cell service. Probably. I smiled.

She finally looked up to realize I was still there. "This is a worthy gift."

"As are all of yours," I said with a smile.

She stood up, gathered something from another one of her tables, and handed it to me.

"A modification of the spell ball I gave you for the house. This should work on the griffin's nest and hold your shadow magic within it to keep it from fading."

"You are a marvel, Dana."

"Hmpf."

I laughed at the sound she made as it copied Mr. Mittens's favorite grunt. Careful not to thank her, I waved goodbye and left her to her toy. Then I went to find the others who'd wandered away once it was clear I was fixed. I guess Goch didn't need to stay. I should probably find him and let him know I was back.

Before I did, Megan found me.

"Dana's amazing," she said.

I agreed.

"Do you think she'll love her phone?"

"I'm thinking next time we are back; Dana will have set up her own cell service and will be charging new customers," I replied with a laugh.

"Probably. I just hope she doesn't have it taken apart so we can use it."

"I probably should have brought her two. One to use, one to take apart and study. I didn't think that one through."

"Portable magic is her thing, not yours. You did great just to make those work here."

"Yeah, I guess. I was going to go tell Goch he doesn't have to hang around. Have you seen him?"

"Goch and I have plans. Don't worry about him," she said.

I stopped and turned to face her. "What do you two have going on?"

"Nothing, I swear. We're just going to explore a little. He likes company, and we've been dying to fly together.

Now that you're on board, we don't have to hide our plans."

I sighed. I didn't own or control anyone. "Why didn't you just tell me?"

"You seemed so against it, but Goch doesn't mind. He likes having a friend around. That's why he got so upset when Mr. Mittens was mad at him. And this is my chance to be a real dragonrider. How many people can say that?"

"You are ridiculous, my friend. But I'm not your keeper or Goch's. I just worry about you, that's all."

"Nothing to worry about."

"You're probably right. Just don't get shot out there. I don't know how the Fae feel about dragons."

"I didn't think they had dragons?"

"Dragons have the ability to realm walk. I'm sure they have myths about dragons."

"We'll be safe and stay out of view, Mom."

I nudged her with my shoulder. "Don't be mean."

"I'll see you at home." She waved and jogged off down a different corridor than the one we'd been walking down.

I headed to my grandfather's den. I had a gift to give him before I could return home to my own issues.

I knocked politely and let myself in.

Grandfather was sitting with Mr. Mittens. They both turned to look as I entered.

"Am I interrupting?"

Mr. Mittens jumped down from the seat he had been in and rubbed against my legs. *All fixed, pet?* he asked.

"Yes, I'm so glad I can hear you again. That was the worst!"

I agree. I'll be more diligent about witches in the future, he promised.

"Yes, no more witches. Although I don't know how to

screen for them if they lie. I'll just make sure to guard my grandparents' books more closely."

Hmpf. Indeed.

"I just need to talk to grandfather quickly, then we can return if you're ready?"

I am ready, pet.

I sat in the chair Mr. Mittens had abandoned and handed my grandfather his gift. Unlike Dana, he'd examined one closely before. The only time she'd seen one was when I'd had her look at it briefly to understand the concept of video recording.

"A cell phone?" he said. "I didn't think these worked on Faerie?"

"It will now. I magicked this one and one for Dana. We can call each other across the realms. No more general alert magic balls."

I showed him how to work it, and what else he could do with it. There wouldn't be internet, but I'd saved a bunch of videos and fun things on both phones. Plus, now they could make their own videos and take pictures without a magical bug being involved.

"I will treasure this gift," he remarked.

I smiled at him. "I'm so glad I met you, Grandfather, and that we could be in each other's lives. I'll call." I held up my phone and wiggled it around.

"I'll be waiting." He smiled.

I turned to Mr. Mittens. "I'm ready."

We walked home.

Chapter Thirty-Two

We hadn't been gone very long, so I didn't time walk. Big mistake. We appeared in the parking lot, which was full of griffins. Mr. Mittens immediately shifted into his Splintercat form. I grabbed onto my magic.

"Hello? Can I help you?" I asked loudly, making my way through the crowd and trying to figure out who I needed to talk to.

The royals finally noticed me and made their way over. I skirted around until the house was at my back, and the griffins were a safe distance. At least I was safe from beaks and claws for a moment. Mr. Mittens stood in front of me, killing teeth bared and fur bristled.

"You are the human we spoke to last time about our son?" the king of the griffins asked.

"I am."

"You lied to us."

I cringed inwardly. "I misled you, that is true, but it wasn't my tale to tell. I immediately let Brightfeather know to contact you, which she did. I'm very sorry for your loss."

The queen hissed at me. I didn't know griffins hissed, but I guess they were half cat. Mr. Mittens started to growl.

"We demand to see Brightfeather immediately."

I nodded. "I will let her know."

"We will wait," he said.

Great. I couldn't lead them to the nest. Should I send my cat? Probably not. He was in protection mode. I told him silently what I was going to do, took a step, and landed at the nest.

"Brightfeather, it's Brigid, and we have a problem."

She stepped out of the nest and looked at me. "They are here."

"Yes."

I reached into my pocket and pulled out Dana's magic ball. "I can hide the nest, but the children would have to be quiet."

"I'll speak to them and let them know we are in danger."

She went back in, and I prepped the magic ball to allow me, Brightfeather, and Mr. Mittens to enter and pulled up my shadow magic. I activated the shield and a momentary shimmer in the air allowed me to see it briefly. I stepped inside, the barrier feeling physical like passing through a bubble, then I was through. I pulled up my shadow magic to fill the space around the nest and make it invisible. The shadows obeyed. By the time Brightfeather exited, nothing could be seen.

"I'm ready," she announced.

I placed my hand on her and walked us.

We appeared in the same spot I'd vacated moments ago.

Brightfeather bowed low before her in-laws.

"We wish to see our son's grave, and you will take us there," they demanded.

Brightfeather looked at me. The spot we'd buried Umber was at the waterfall, the place of my power, and I didn't allow just anyone there. I nodded. "It will be fine. Go ahead."

She thanked me and leapt into the air, her strong wings lifting her above the trees in seconds. The rest of the griffins did the same, and they banked and headed toward the waterfall. I wondered if I should accompany them, but the royals weren't happy with me currently. They had a right to attend their son's grave. I ducked into the house, Mr. Mittens back in Ragdoll form and clinging to my ankles. He wasn't going to let me out of his sight as long as the griffins were around and a threat.

I wondered if they'd asked her if she had produced eggs or chicks. How would she get away with that level of lie? I guess it wasn't my problem. I'd agreed to keep the chicks safe, and I was going the best I could, keeping them hidden. Did I agree with her decision? No. I understood not wanting to give up your children, but I figured that Bright-feather and the royals could compromise. The royals should be allowed to see their grandchildren, and the children deserved to know their father's family as well. But that wasn't my call to make.

I ran upstairs to check on Gabe and the witch—Sofia's younger sister.

I opened the door. Gabe was sitting in the chair. He looked up at me and smiled. "Did it work?"

"Yes, Dana is a marvel. However, she doubts that what she did would free the witch. She'd have to come and do it deliberately, and she won't."

He nodded. "I'll check her again, see if the block is gone. It might have been tied to the spell blocking you."

It was worth a chance.

He laid his hands on her head, and I watched his face as he concentrated. He shook his head. "The block remains."

"I don't know what to do. Should I call a hospital?"

"Yes. We should have her transported, and then whatever happens is not attached to you."

"I should be angrier at her. She tried to steal my magic, she lied to me, and she stole my grandmother's books." I looked down at her. "I guess she has punished herself enough."

I pulled out my phone and called 911.

"Nine-one-one, what's your emergency?" the generic voice intoned.

"I have a guest at my inn who is nonresponsive. We need an ambulance."

I gave them my address, my name, and her name. Although they wanted me to stay on the line, I hung up.

"I guess that's it," I said.

"I'll stay with her; you can meet the EMTs."

"Yeah, good idea." I looked around. We'd picked up the spell implements and the books, but the painted floor was still visible. I found the rug that she'd kicked into a corner and laid it over the spell circle. Some paint was visible along the edges, but I couldn't do anything about that.

"Do I need to tell them anything or leave that to you?" I asked.

"I can reassure them that I believe she had a stroke. She has enough symptoms similar to it that it's entirely possible."

"Do you think there will be a problem since I called you first and not the ambulance?"

He shrugged. "They don't know the timeline. For all they know, I was here when we heard her fall, and after examining her, we called the ambulance immediately."

I guess made-up facts were good. We couldn't tell them she burned herself out magically and used her life-force to try to steal my magic. We'd be laughed at and charged for attempted murder. Stroke it was.

I could hear the sirens in the distance, so I gave Gabe a quick kiss and hurried downstairs to meet them. I sure hoped the griffins stayed gone until the ambulance left. I wasn't sure how to explain that to regular humans.

On my way down the stairs, over the sirens, I heard Goch's trumpeting to let us know he and Megan had returned. Good. One less worry.

Chapter Thirty-Three

I sent Mr. Mittens to check on the griffins while we waited for the ambulance. Finally, it came streaking up the long drive and backed up to the front door. That seemed odd to me since there was so much more room around back. I opened the door, and the EMTs opened the back of the ambulance to pull out a gurney.

I waited, ready to invite them in to retrieve the witch, but they gave themselves away. As the one EMT leaned over to grab a medical bag, he let a little fang show. I wouldn't have seen it, but it happened to catch the dim light from the porch lamps.

I reeled back and slammed the door. "Madison!" I gasped.

She rounded the desk.

I looked at her. "Call your brother; we have vampires."

She snatched her phone out of her back pocket. I saw her hit a few buttons, and then, "Noah, we're under attack. Yeah. Vamps. OK." She hung up.

I didn't hear Noah's side, but I could gather that he was

coming. Hopefully with a lot of wolves. Just then, the EMT started pounding on the door. "EMTs, we're here for the patient."

I looked through the thin glass partitions that lined the door. The glass was pretty, but not very safe. Anyone could break in with enough desire. Four vamps. My palms began to sweat.

I called Mr. Mittens silently.

They are still here, he said. Thinking I was checking on the griffins.

No, we have vampires. Hurry back! I called silently.

Hmpf.

Even though that was his annoyed sound, I could feel the worry in his mental voice. Plus, it was followed by a pulse of power as he realm walked to get here sooner.

Sure enough, he appeared at my side seconds later.

How many? he asked.

"I only see four, but I think they are alerted that we're on to them now, and I don't know how many more they could be calling in or that are hidden in the woods."

I heard a car come up the long drive. "Shit, someone is out there."

I'll go look, Mr. Mittens said. *It could be more vamps.*

He ran to the back to check the parking lot.

Not vamps, he said mentally, *it's your kitsune guests, the whole family.*

My heart fell. They weren't my favorite people, but they had three small children. I couldn't leave them out there with who knew how many vampires—the bloodthirsty monsters. The poor family wouldn't stand a chance.

I ran to my room, unlocked it, and found my bag of magic fireballs. Gabe came down the stairs.

"I thought the ambulance was here?"

"It is, only it's being driven by vampires."

He looked shocked. I handed him the bag. "Defend yourself."

"How many are out there?"

"Unknown, but Mr. Mittens is out there. I have guests out there, too. A family of five, the children are all under eight."

He clenched the bag tightly. "Let's go get them in the house."

I nodded and pulled my magic up, so it was ready. We raced to the back.

It seemed quiet out back, no one but the Kitsune family back from picking their kids up from camp. The parents were getting out and wrangling children towards the house. The mom, Tomiko, looked at me with a question, but I just waved as though nothing was wrong and continued to search for vampires.

Unless Vic Constantine had called in favors with other old vamps, I knew all he had left were his scrubs—his young vamps under a hundred years without the ability to withstand the sun, and without the mastery to change into the massive man-bat form that had terrorized Megan and haunted my dreams. However, the light was fading, and as usual it was heavily overcast, which meant that the daring young ones, sure that no stray sunbeam would erupt and devour them, would feel free to move about.

The family was finally all out of the car and making their way to the house. I scanned the surrounding trees. There. A pale face peaked out, and fangs were bared. I gave a double take. "Bella?"

She stepped out from the trees and was back to her young, beautiful self. I glanced at the family. "Don't be alarmed, but get in the house now!" I said firmly.

The parents looked at me in alarm.

"Vampires."

They scooped up the children and ran to the house.

Bella and at least ten other vampires stepped out of the trees. Where were my baincallan? How did the vamps get close to the house so quickly?

Bella approached.

"Why, Bella? You had your chance to escape and start a new life?"

"A life as a woman in an aging body?" she scoffed. "I wouldn't wish that on my worst enemy." She ran her hands down her body. "I'm forever young and strong again."

"What about being a new vamp? Don't you have to go a hundred years before you can enjoy all the privileges?"

She bared her teeth at me. "Yes, you ruined that for me. But a hundred years is a drop in the bucket, and I'm still my master's favorite. One last job, and I'm fully back in his good graces. He even promised me that your blood will restore me sooner." She grinned, her fangs glistening white against her olive skin and blood-red lips.

Great. Now she wanted my blood. What was it with the witches and vampires, constantly trying to take everything from me? I should have staked her instead of having Gabe save her from herself. She was too far gone to take the gift she'd been given, anyway.

The kitsune family was safely inside. Gabe stood at my side, and Mr. Mittens was close.

"Remember, the woman is mine!" Bella yelled, and the vampires attacked.

Chapter Thirty-Four

Bella transformed. She couldn't do full man-bat anymore, but she shifted into a regular bat and flew over my head. I didn't have time to watch her to see where she went, because the others, in blinding vamp speed, were upon us. Gabe threw fireballs, and two vamps went up—infernos that burned so hot, the vamps were nothing but ash.

I put up my hands and shot out two lightning bolts. One caught a vamp, but the other was too fast and skirted around it. I blasted my own new car. I cringed. Damn. I was going through cars like chocolate. I was well off, but this was crazy. I couldn't blame an awkward teen dragon for this one, either.

Two vamps skirted around us and headed towards the back door into the kitchen. Several bats flew overhead, and vampires transformed on the roof. They were going to break in. What happened to the invitation thing? No one I knew had invited a vampire into the house after my one guest.

"Shit," I said out loud as the memory hit me like the

lightning bolts I was throwing out. Madison or Megan had invited Bella into the house when she'd delivered a message —I'd forgotten.

Could she get the others in based on her invitation? The sound of breaking glass on the second floor answered my question. I threw a lightning blast, and used the moment to look up to see which window was broken. Damn, it was the witch's room. She was unprotected up there.

Bats were flying in the house like a black cloud. The few left that we were battling suddenly transformed and flew up to join the others.

Mr. Mittens bounded out of the trees, a vamp in his mouth. He bit it in two, and it turned to ash. He took five large bounds and leapt on the roof, chasing the bats. My heart skipped a beat.

We turned and charged in through the kitchen to try to stop them.

Gabe couldn't use the fireballs in the house, or we'd set the whole thing on fire, and I couldn't use lightning—it was too unpredictable, even if I was careful, and my fire magic was out unless it was extremely controlled.

We ran through the house and warned everyone. Chef Jack started stripping off his clothes when we ran past, and when we hit the reception, Madison was already half through her change. Megan stood at the base of the stairs, weapons out, looking up to the second floor. No bats were visible yet.

"The kitsunes?" I asked, "Are they safe?"

Megan tilted her head to my drawing room. "They're in there."

"Where's Goch?"

"He went back to hunt in Faerie with his wyvern friend."

I nodded, but wished he were still here to help.

I noticed that the sidelights to the doors were broken, and no vamps remained outside.

"Where are the EMT vamps?" I asked.

"They went upstairs with the gurney," Megan said.

"What are they doing up there?" I asked rhetorically. I doubted anyone knew.

Megan shrugged. Madison finished her shift and stalked over to join Megan. Her large wolf body stood as tall as Megan's waist. They stood ready at the base of the stairs.

There was a series of thumps and bangs and a swarm of bats fluttered around. A flurry of movement showed Mr. Mittens dusting vamps by the dozens on the second floor.

"Here we go," Megan said and twirled her sword once to limber up her wrist.

The EMT vamps were at the top of the stairs with the gurney, the witch tied down on it. I squinted in confusion at the scene. I couldn't get my head around it. Why were they taking her? She was a burnt-out husk with hardly enough life in her to last the next few days. They looked back at Mr. Mittens, panic in their eyes, and hurried to move the gurney down.

They had the high ground, so we waited at the bottom to defend the drawing room with the vulnerable fox family inside.

The EMTs started down the stairs, which was dumb. I had an elevator, but they probably didn't know or didn't want to go through Mr. Mittens to get into it. Bats flitted everywhere. I was glad my angel couple had left, but that meant we still had one occupied guest room upstairs, the older shifter couple.

"Megan, are the Jorgenson's upstairs or out?"

"Upstairs, or in the dining room."

My eyes flicked to the back. Chef Jack in his tiger form was padding through the swinging doors from the kitchen. He bore a large cat grin.

I wanted to ask Madison how soon it would be before her pack arrived, but she was past speech, and the vampires were on us, anyway. Half stayed in bat form, diving and biting. I threw up a shield of shadow magic, rendering us invisible, but we were still in the same spots, and bats apparently could see quite well in shadows. Paired with their echolocation, we were as visible as before. After the bats proved they could get through, I dropped the shadows; it made it hard for us to see one another. Megan slapped a bat out of the air with her shield and removed its head with her sword in almost a single smooth motion. It burst into dust.

I caught another with a burst of flame, and when it started to fall to my floor, I sent a burst of magic at it, and it disappeared. I looked around but couldn't spend too much thought on it or where it went. The bats were swarming Gabe. He appeared to be the most vulnerable, since he didn't bear a visible weapon. What they didn't know was that he wasn't unarmed. He snatched two bats out of the air. His warm magic pulsed out, and two humans slipped to the ground, unconscious and healed of vampirism.

Their fellows fell on them and began biting and licking up blood. Once they landed on the bodies, we could slaughter them easier, and black and grey bat bodies soon lay everywhere. They weren't dead, since none turned to dust, but we'd taken several out of the fight for a short time. When I got a break, I'd dispatch the bats, along with everyone else.

The gurney clattered to the floor. I whirled at the sound. Only one EMT remained. He'd managed to keep the gurney upright, and the witch bound on it was still unconscious. Mr. Mittens snapped his teeth on the third of the four and it turned into ash. The other left the gurney, turned, and ran for the door. That was a mistake with a large predator. Mr. Mittens sprinted, and in one mighty pounce, he caught the vamp one step from the broken side-lights. With a single snap of his jaws, it was dust.

There were just so many. Even with the six of us dispatching vamps rapidly, there were always more.

We were all bleeding from various bat bites, except for Mr. Mittens. He would snap, slash, and rip bats to shreds before they burst into dust. The rest of us weren't as quick, and bats would inevitably get through to bite us.

Tiger Jack finally got around us and fought his way up the stairs, where almost all the vamps had entered. Mr. Mittens saw what he was doing and joined him, heading back up, the two large cats mincing bats as they battled their way through.

The bats around us on the ground floor were thinning. The cats had pushed the bulk of the bats back. Megan started up after them. Gabe rushed over to check on the witch, still strapped to the gurney. Weirdly, no bats attempted to bite her. I was shocked. What did the vamps want with her? What was the deal?

"She's the same, stable," Gabe reported.

I wasn't sure what to do with her. Whatever the vamps wanted, we definitely shouldn't give to them. I shoved the gurney over to my drawing room door. Surely, she'd be safe there with the kitsune family? The bats were still around, but much thinner. I didn't want to let any in with the vulnerable children, so after I unlocked the door. Gabe got ready to push the gurney in, while I swept the bats away with gusts of air.

"I'm ready."

"On three?"

"Yes."

"One, two, three!" He shoved the gurney through, and I blasted the bats back. He closed the door, and I relocked it. We'd kept the room vampire bat free. We bumped fists.

I turned to follow Megan, Madison, and the two cats up the stairs. They were making better time and were nearly halfway up. As I stepped forward to join them, a bat fluttered in front of me and shifted into Bella.

She glared at me.

"What do you want?" I asked.

She folded her arms across her chest. "We want you and all your friends to die."

"Shame."

She smirked. "We might consider a truce if you hand over the witch."

"How long of a truce?" My mind raced. Could the witch harm us if we gave her up? I glanced at Gabe, who was shaking his head. He wouldn't give her to the vamps because he was a good man and wouldn't give a helpless person up to bloodsuckers. Could I?

"We can discuss terms."

"One hundred years," I snapped out.

She barked out a laugh. "A hundred? Never going to happen. How about one?"

"No, you want her for some reason, badly. So, pay up. Seventy-five."

She scoffed. "We'll never give you so many, be realistic. Five?"

"Fifty, final offer."

"That is too much. I must consult my master."

"Then take your minions and consult."

She glared at me a moment, then shifted back to her bat

and flew out the sidelight. She didn't stop the battle or take anyone, of course. She was nasty like that.

Brigid, we are returning. Brightfeather's mental voice interrupted my internal hate filled rant.

Well, shit. I had a vampire battle, and sad, angry griffins. What else could possibly happen?

I heard a truck racing up my long drive. I sure hoped it was the werewolves. Gabe and I headed out the back to meet the griffins, while the others battled the vampires in the house. I hoped Noah brought lots of reinforcements, and where were my baincallan? I was worried now—Sorcha was intense, and she wouldn't leave us to face this alone if something weren't wrong.

A few bats chased us down the corridor, but without shifting or more numbers, they couldn't follow us through the heavy swinging doors. Once through, we made better time and finally burst out the back. I looked at the house. It was engulfed in a black cloud of bats. I wanted to scream, but that would draw their attention to us. Right now, they were focused on gaining entry to the house.

Noah burst out of the driver's side of his truck, Luke and Michael went out the other side, and several wolves—already shifted—bounded out of the back.

Luke raced over to us. "Where do you need us the most?"

"The others are battling from the inside, trying to drive the vamps back out. We also have the griffins coming back from the waterfall, and the baincallan are missing. Can one of you check on them?"

"I will," Michael said.

I thanked him, and he stripped, shifted, and ran off towards the dairy.

Swirling air from griffin wings battered the bats and disrupted them for a few moments.

"What is this?" the griffin king demanded after he landed.

"We are under attack by vampires." I felt like I was stating the obvious, but he'd asked.

"Are these the vampires that killed my son?"

I looked around. The vampires had finally noticed that there were potential victims outside again, and some had zeroed in on us.

"Yes." I sent a lightning bolt at one and fried it in the air. Several, now that there was space, started shifting into their human forms, and were racing at us.

Megan yelled down from the open window upstairs. "We have them out. Set the barrier!"

Crap, I forgot about the barrier. I shoved my hands in my pockets, but it wasn't there. I'd stashed it in my drawer at some point.

"They deserve to die!" The griffin king yelled.

The griffins exploded outward, some in the air chasing bats, and the rest using their vicious beaks and talons on the ground.

I whirled and ran into the house to get my ball to keep the vamps out of the house.

I swiped my key card and threw open my bedroom door, racing to my dresser. I pocketed the barrier ball, grabbed everything else just in case, and raced back to the melee. I stumbled out the door with everyone else. Megan, the werewolves, Mr. Mittens, and Jack joined the fray, and finally we were starting to beat back the vampires. I sent the few bats closest to the house flying with gusts of air while concentrating on who could enter and leave the house. I threw the ball to the ground and stomped on it to activate it.

A great whoosh sounded, and the force of the barrier rising displaced the air all around and threw us backward. I landed hard on my bottom and groaned. Gabe caught himself and gracefully landed on his feet. The shifters were fine, even if they were rolled around a bit, and Mr. Mittens gave a horrible, angry yowl, but didn't stop attacking bats. The griffins just seemed to lift up in the air and land smoothly if they were on the ground.

I didn't see Megan, but the string of swearing was a hint that she'd also been caught off guard and tossed around.

I assumed the force that had displaced air around the house proved that the barrier was up and running, and I was rewarded by a vampire, being thrown through the air by a swat from Mr. Mittens, striking it and sliding down it while bursting into flames. That Dana was an evil genius.

"Be careful around the barrier. It will set you on fire if you aren't authorized!" I yelled, mainly for the griffins. I had authorized my guests, the baincallan, my cat, the Whelans, Megan, and Chef Jack.

The fight shifted close to the woods. Several vamps in both forms had gone up in flames on contact with the barrier, and they were wary. But more and more bats and vampires in human form were appearing from the woods. True dark had fallen now, and they weren't holding back.

My magic was singing, the thrill of using it burning through me like whiskey. I sent flames and lightning bolts at bats and human vamps, and they exploded in flames. Some just disappeared, though I wasn't sure what was happening, and I didn't have time to explore.

The griffins were fierce in battle, and what little I had time to watch amazed me and terrified me at the same time.

If they turned on us and attacked, we wouldn't stand a chance.

A griffin next to me gripped a vamp in its viciously sharp talons and neatly bit its head off with its sharp beak. The vamp exploded into dust after the heart was pierced by brutal talons.

The magic was burning me up. I started to sweat. I'd never used this much at once, even under Dana's tutelage. The lightning was branching out of me and zapping several vamps at once. I was starting to fear that I would hit one of my allies.

Mr. Mittens bumped me accidentally, and I fell under one of the griffins. I couldn't see which one, but I had to rein in my magic to keep from hurting it. I tried. It was like a raging river, and I tried to dam it with only my will. I didn't know what was wrong. It had never done this to me before. It was like I overfilled on Fae magic, and it had to be released or I would explode.

If I did it here, I'd hurt everyone. I rolled away, regained my feet, and headed toward the waterfall. I passed through the invisible barrier hiding the trail, and tried to force my legs to move faster, to get away. I panted and clasped my arms around my belly to hold it in. I had to make it far enough away. I partially walked, partially ran to the spring. Water. Maybe it would cool the burning path of the magic that pulsed through me with every beat of my heart. I stuck my face in it and sucked down the cold, clear water. It eased my parched throat but didn't stop the burning.

The magic was pulsing harder now, and I couldn't hold it back much longer. I raced to the top of the trail to the waterfall, seeking the safety at the core of my power. I stood on my favorite boulder, feeling the link from Faerie to my land. And finally, I let my magic go.

A mighty pulse of power shot out in every direction. It appeared to me as a white light and swept outward like the ripples in a pond. I screamed with the release. Exhausted, I wilted to the stone. Nothing like that had ever happened. I wondered if it was a result of the witch's spell, or if it would happen again if I overused my power. I felt drained, but not fully empty, and the link was trying to refresh my power even as I lay still on the stone, trying to slow my breath and control my panic.

Brigid? Mr. Mittens mental voice echoed in my mind.

Yes?

Come back to the house. You need to be here.

I don't know if I can walk that far.

Then walk.

I knew he meant realm walk. Could I? I'd just expended a ton of power. But when I sat up, I felt refreshed and renewed. The power hummed, not painful or burning as it felt before, but like the purr of a perfectly tuned engine. A vibration along my nerves. I took a deep breath and stepped to the practice planet on route to the house.

I looked around in shock at the field on the practice planet where we usually arrived. It was littered with vampires in bat and human form. I nudged one with my foot, but it didn't move. It hadn't turned to dust, so I wasn't sure if they were dead, but they were completely unmoving. I grabbed a bat, pinched its wing between forefinger and thumb and held it out from my body, then finished my walk back to the house.

When I arrived, the bat turned to dust in my fingers. How odd. I shook my head. I'd wonder about that later.

Mr. Mittens huffed and got my attention. I looked around. Everyone, including my cat, was frozen in place. Some were even frozen, suspended off the ground.

"Can you move?" I asked my cat.

No.

"What happened?" I asked.

A pulse of white light ripped through, and everything it touched froze in place, he answered.

My heart stopped. This was me? My magic? "Something is wrong with my magic."

I looked around. Maybe I should go through and end all vamps before I tried to unfreeze my friends.

"What do I do?" I asked out loud, not really expecting an answer.

Turn it off, free us, Mr. Mittens said.

I looked around. Then I concentrated on my cat to see if I could unfreeze him. He was in the motion of trying to rip a head off a vamp, and it looked painful to be stuck in that pose, his body twisted with the force he was about to use.

I concentrated and told my magic to let him go. His motion completed, and he dropped to all fours, the dust of the vamp drifting to the ground.

Before I could free the others, Mr. Mittens swept through the vamps like wildfire, decimating their numbers. Finally, I'd released everyone, and the fighting resumed. Only, the vamps saw the writing on the wall and fled into the night on wings and feet.

Wolf Michael raced into the parking lot as the last of the vamps melted away. He shifted. "Brigid, we need everyone at the dairy; they've been attacked as well."

My heart dropped.

Chapter Thirty-Five

"What is this?" the griffin king roared.

"I have to go, sorry," I said and raced to the edge of the parking lot. I stopped. What was I thinking? I could realm walk there faster. The wolves were close on my heels, as were Gabe, Megan, Chef Jack, and Mr. Mittens.

I glanced at my cat, and a silent understanding passed between us, and then we both walked.

Mr. Mittens and I landed in the closest field to the dairy and ran to the gate. He simply leaped over it, but I used the gate and ran towards the building where the baincallan were housed. My friends would be here soon. It took maybe ten to fifteen minutes to walk here briskly, and I bet some of them would run.

We both skidded to a stop outside the building. Jim, in his shifted Quetzalcoatl form, was nailed to the outside of the building. I gasped, and my hand covered my mouth involuntarily. The beautiful rainbow-colored feathered serpent hung limply, two giant nails driven through his body, one right below his head, and the other in his tail.

I ran up to him. He was breathing shallowly. I grabbed a nail and realized I couldn't budge it. Jim couldn't speak. I wasn't even sure he was conscious. It was best to wait for Gabe, anyway; he'd need a healer if someone could pull the nails from the building without further damage. I left Mr. Mittens to guard him and barged into the building, dreading what I would see.

Blood was splashed everywhere, and two baincallan, obviously the ones on break, lay on the floor, limp and lifeless. The bodies had been savaged by vampire bat teeth, and other than the splashes of blood indicating a battle, they were drained and pale.

Where were the other four? Would I find them dead in my woods? Where was my friend, Sorcha? My heart fluttered, and my throat closed off with grief. I'd brought them here to die. What was I thinking?

I don't know how long I stood staring in shock, but I heard my name called and rushed out to guide my friends to us. Mr. Mittens stayed firm and fierce, guarding Jim.

"Over here, hurry!" I yelled out.

The wolves and Jack were first, since they were in animal form. Gabe and Megan brought up the rear. They must have run, and the others must have held back some to keep them protected.

"It's Jim," I said, a sob tearing out of my throat.

Luke shifted after seeing the nails and ran for the tool shed. Gabe finally reached me and carefully placed his hands on Jim.

I sent Jack and the wolves to look for the other baincallan.

"It's bad. If we can remove the nails, I think I can keep him stable. We need him to shift, though. I think I'll have a better chance of healing him if he's human."

Megan reached me and pulled me into a hug. I couldn't do anything at this point. I could only watch.

"Wait!" I yelled, shocking even myself. "I have this!" I pulled out one of the healing balls I'd placed in my pocket earlier. I handed it to Gabe. "Do you think it will help?"

He looked at it. His gift was phenomenal, but I'd seen Dana's healing balls bring people back from the brink more than once. And they weren't creature specific. They'd healed a griffin before.

"It can't hurt. We'll have to pull the nails first."

I looked at the first nail, it was just below his head, blocking the throat. The tears slid down my face unchecked.

Luke was back with a pry bar and hammer. It looked like it would be brutal to remove the large nails from the small body. I wanted to turn my back. I didn't want to watch, but it was my battle, my fault, so I forced myself for Jim's sake—to be there for him.

Gabe kept a hand on Jim's head, and Luke started on the nail in his tail first. He placed the pry bar and whacked it with the hammer. It took three hits before he could pull it free of his body. Jim struggled weakly, still unaware, his body reacting.

Luke wiped his forehead, the stress of the action and knowing he could damage Jim further showing on his face. He gulped and placed the pry bar again. This time, he did it in two hits. Gabe caught the serpent's body and set it gently on the ground.

The serpent's mouth was open. Gabe, working carefully around his venom filled fangs, pushed the healing ball to the back of Jim's mouth, and then he stroked his throat to move it down. It slipped down. He kept his hand on the serpent, monitoring him.

"He's not breathing," he announced.

A sob caught in my throat.

There was no way to give him CPR. I didn't even know where a heart on a feathered serpent was. Looking around, everyone else was as helpless as me. Except Gabe. He was a doctor and a healer. He kept his hands on Jim, and I felt the warmth of his magic surround the serpent.

Whether it was Dana's healing ball or Gabe's magic, the serpent twitched.

"He's breathing," Gabe announced. We all took a breath, then looked at each other, nervous titters breaking out.

The serpent blurred, and Jim lay on the ground in human form. The wound in the center of his chest looked like someone had driven a pole through him, but it was closing. Gabe closed his eyes, his hands never leaving Jim.

"The magic ball is working; I can see his internal organs healing."

We waited to see if he would awaken, but before he did, my nemesis appeared.

She walked towards me from behind the building, hips swaying as though she owned the place.

Mr. Mittens hissed. I put myself between her and Jim, and Mr. Mittens stood to my right. Megan, weapons ready, stood to my left.

"I'm here for the witch," she said.

"Why? She's more than half dead, and there's no saving her." I wasn't in the mood for beating around the bush.

"She'll live, particularly once she's turned."

"What is she to you? Why her?"

She shrugged. "That's not your business."

"It is if you want her back."

"Touché." She sighed and waved her hand, indicating

that she didn't care. "Fine. My master has a personal interest in her."

I frowned. "Personal? You mean like a girlfriend?"

"Or his wife."

"Wife?!"

They'd really played us. I felt like I'd been punched in the gut. Luckily, Megan had her wits about her.

"So, you want her back rather desperately. We'll take those hundred years of peace."

Bella shook her head. "No. We'll give you a year."

"No deal, get lost. We'll make her comfortable until the end, and you can collect her ashes," Megan added with a sneer.

Bella snarled at us. "We will take her back; you can't stop us. We have your warriors."

I stiffened and grabbed Megan's arm.

"Are they alive?"

Bella shrugged. "For now, but their blood is so delicious, it's invigorating." She smiled a toothy grin and shivered with delight.

Mr. Mittens growled, and I wished I had a stake.

"Fine, we'll trade. The four baincallan for your witch."

She smiled. "I thought you'd see things my way."

I looked over at my friends, hurt and exhausted, and I thought of my two dead. "Bring them to the house. We'll trade there. I wouldn't take too long; she doesn't have much time."

Bella nodded and shifted away into the night. Her triumphant smile would haunt me for a long time.

Chapter Thirty-Six

Gabe and Luke helped Jim into his house. Gabe offered to stay, but Jim waved him off, saying that he was fine. After examining him thoroughly, Gabe agreed and told him to rest. Jack and the wolves were back, so Jack stayed, since he lived there, and said he'd check on Jim through the night. The wolves ran back to the house where their clothes were, and Gabe, Megan, Mr. Mittens, and I walked back.

The barrier was still humming along my nerve endings, so I knew it remained active. I reached out to touch it gingerly, checking that my suggestions worked before I allowed anyone to pass through it. It was fine. It tingled when we walked through, but no one was repelled or burst into flames.

We walked into the house. The kitchen was messy but regular messy. The rest of the house was a mess. I'd had everything repaired and redecorated after the poltergeist incident months ago, and it looked as though I'd have to do it again.

My dismay must have shown on my face because Gabe hugged me and attempted to reassure me.

I didn't know what to do. The vampires had won this round. I still had to deal with the griffins, which were thankfully gone, and I'd probably offended them on top of getting their son killed.

We stumbled our way to the drawing room. I unlocked the door. The kitsunes and the gurney were still inside. The two older children were on my sofa, sleeping. The parents were in opposite chairs, Mrs. Nishiyama holding her sleeping toddler.

"Is it over?" she asked, quietly.

I nodded. "Your room is safe. You can go back. You might want to take the elevator—there's a lot of wreckage. I'm so sorry."

She didn't say anything but started out the door. I figured I'd hear it from them one way or another, but I was too exhausted to worry about it now. The father woke up the boy and picked up his daughter. They left us alone with the witch.

Gabe laid his hands on her. "Same."

I felt a little wave of relief. I doubted my baincallan friends would survive if the witch did not.

"We'll have to take her out past the barrier, or they won't be able to take her," I stated, even though he knew.

He just nodded. "I'll have the Whelans help me."

I didn't have the energy to do much more than nod.

Mr. Mittens had shrunk back down to this Ragdoll shape, but he was patrolling the house to make sure all the vampire bats were indeed out. We couldn't leave a single one left within. The witch's broken window would have to be replaced, but for now, we just shut the door. We'd have to clean up the wreckage the battle had left before we could relax, but first we had the trade to make. I didn't know how long the vamps would take before they returned to make the trade.

The Whelans were waiting for us in the front. Gabe had Noah, Luke, and Michael take a hold of the gurney. The four of them pushed the gurney out, carried it down the front steps, and pushed it into the waiting ambulance which had been left behind. Then, we waited.

A short, startled scream from inside the house had us rush back in. Madison was behind the desk, straightening up from the battle. She was staring down at something. I rounded the desk to see what it was. Mr. Mittens jumped up on it so he could protect me.

A bat lay on the floor.

"I stabbed it through the heart, but it won't turn to dust," she said. It obviously worried and disturbed her.

"That's not good. Must be some kind of super vampire," I replied.

It is just a bat. I left it there to have as a snack, Mr. Mittens added, before jumping down and munching the bat in a few bites.

I translated for Madison.

"Dammit, cat," Madison said. "You almost gave me a heart attack. You have to warn a person who's just been through a vampire bat battle."

It wasn't a vampire bat, only an ordinary one, he said, confused.

I choked a little on my laughter when I told her what he'd said.

"Well, I didn't examine it. I just stabbed it," Madison said, annoyed.

Hmpf. If appropriate snacks are provided, I wouldn't have to leave my own laying around, Mr. Mittens said. *I need to eat to be the magnificent killer that I am.*

I gave him a sharp look, but he insisted I say it to Madison.

"What snacks do you consider appropriate?" Madison asked him.

"You do not want to go there," I warned. "You'll be spending all of your income supplying him premium snacks. Just let it go."

Madison snort-laughed, and Mr. Mittens huffed.

We heard a vehicle. This must be it, the exchange. We hurried outside to the porch, within the barrier, but close enough to control the ambulance and its occupant. Gabe and the Whelan brothers had stood watch while we were inside dealing with Madison's panicked scream.

A black limousine came up the drive. The windows were tinted so dark, they appeared black. I doubted they'd pass the window tint laws in this state.

Everyone went quiet and waited. We didn't trust the vamps. However, if the witch, June or Amber, was Vic Constantine's wife, this might have more weight. We stood ready for anything.

The limo stopped behind the ambulance. In truth, the space in front of the porch didn't have room for another vehicle. At least they'd blocked themselves from stealing the ambulance with the witch inside.

The rear door opened, and Bella and Vic climbed out. I strained to see if my baincallan were inside, but the vamps blocked the view.

They passed behind the ambulance and turned to face us.

"Don't come closer. The house is protected by a barrier that doesn't like vamps," I warned. "Where are my friends?"

Vic lifted a hand, and another vampire exited the front of the limo, and opened the rear door. Four Amazonian sized women were pulled out and shoved roughly against the car, their hands bound and cloth bags over their faces.

"Remove the bags," Vic commanded.

The vamp removed the bags from each woman. The women leaned or braced themselves against the car, obviously weak and anemic.

Sorcha glared at the vamps, and if her hands were free, my money said she'd find a way to kill them. They had to have taken her and the others by surprise or overwhelming numbers.

"We held up our end. Where's Amber?" Vic asked.

I gave a head nod towards the ambulance. "She is inside, very weak and frail, but currently alive. Push the four women over towards us, so they pass inside the barrier, and we'll walk inside and let you take her and the ambulance.

He flicked his fingers at his vamp minions, and they roughly pulled the women around the ambulance and shoved them towards the front porch. The baincallan stumbled up the few steps and inside the barrier. Once they were all in, we helped them inside the house and watched from the broken sidelights as Vic checked on his wife, and then both vehicles drove back down the drive and away.

Only when I couldn't see their taillights anymore did I breathe a sigh of relief. We sat the baincallan women down in the drawing room, and Gabe examined them, healing bites and bruises and other wounds. Once he was done, I went into the kitchen and heated up food for them. Food and drink would help them replenish their missing blood, which healing could accelerate but not replace.

"They killed Fain and Sera, didn't they?" Sorcha asked as she ate.

"Yes."

She nodded, but her eyes were haunted. "Did they kill a bunch of the bloodsuckers first?"

They'd been surprised, but I wanted her to have peace of mind. "Yes. They went down fighting."

"Good."

She continued to eat. As a soldier, you ate, drank, and slept when you could because you never knew when you'd get a chance again. I respected that. I'd be wallowing in my grief, but wallowing didn't solve anything.

Maybe I was finally learning to compartmentalize, because I shoved the grief I felt at losing the two warriors into a corner. I was attempting to ignore it until later. I was responsible, I knew it, but I couldn't let it distract me now.

"What happened?" I asked Sorcha.

"They caught us by surprise."

I'd figured that, but she needed a moment to figure out how to explain.

"We were in a rotation through the woods. We were keeping watch, but apparently not good enough watch on the skies. It was dark in the canopy, and next thing I know I'm waking up, trussed up with a bag on my head."

"I'm so sorry I put you and your fellows in harm's way. I shouldn't have asked you to come. It's too dangerous."

She snorted. "It's what we do. It's our choice to work as soldiers. We are good at it, better than most. I'd like to think we were doing a good job. We'll do better now. They'll never get the drop on us."

"Are you sure? You've lost two, and you're shorthanded. You won't hurt my feelings if you want to go home."

"No. I'll call for reinforcements. We'll stay. The blood-suckers have made a fatal mistake by releasing us."

I wasn't sure if I felt horrified or relieved that they were staying. I had caused the death of two sentient creatures that were helping me. That was big. At the same time, I needed the help or more of my people would die.

One thing was sure. I was going to have to close the inn. I'd already lost one couple to the vampires; I was a fool to think I could protect anyone that stayed here.

I left Sorcha and her warriors to finish their meal and pulled the Whelans, Megan, and Gabe together.

"This isn't sustainable. We can't protect the guests, and you guys have to keep saving me and the house. It's time to close the inn, maybe time to leave altogether."

There were a bunch of shocked faces, then everyone began talking at once.

It was Mr. Mittens's voice that superseded the others, since he spoke directly into my mind.

I will always keep you safe.

I looked down at him with love. "I know, my friend. Thank you."

He rubbed on my legs.

"So, Madison and Megan, can you start contacting the guests with reservations, and I'll go make an announcement on the website that we had some kind of issue and need to close for repairs or something."

Madison looked stricken. She really liked the job here, and I didn't want to lose her, Jack, or Jim as employees. I'd have to find something for them to do until I could figure out a long-term solution for the vamp problem.

I was too tired to think about it now. Tomorrow.

Tomorrow the guests would leave, and we'd cancel the others. Then I'd have room to breathe and space to figure out my next steps. First, we needed to finish the basic cleanup so the guests could leave safely, then I had repairs to arrange after.

Gabe put his arm around me. For a non-mind reader, he did a good job of knowing what I was thinking and why. He leaned down and kissed the top of my head. "This too will pass."

I smiled up at him. "It will. We'll figure it out tomorrow."

I wasn't sure I felt much hope, but it was nice to pretend for others.

Everyone set to work cleaning up debris. I felt so much gratitude because I knew they were as tired as I was. After it was safe for the guests, the Whelans headed home, except Luke, who followed Megan upstairs. Gabe had to work and left me on the porch with a scorching kiss.

Soon, it was me and Mr. Mittens standing on the back porch together. "What do we do now?" I asked. "Any advice?"

He leaned against me. *Well pet, I only see one choice. We go to their home and clean them out forever.*

I bent down and rubbed his ears. "I like the way you think. But you can't leave this land."

Then we'll find a way I can, pet. He sat and wrapped his floofy tail around his feet. Looking at him in this form amused me as I thought about his words. No one would think a super-charged killing machine lived in his fancy, long-haired housecat body. I stood up taller; no one would believe that of me either, especially if they'd seen the timid, scared, over-trusting mess I'd been when I'd started this journey.

I thought of the vampires, how we'd nearly decimated them, and if they hadn't checked us by kidnapping the baincallan, we'd have had a real truce. We were close to a win there. We had to be. Of course, the griffins were another problem to worry about, but right now, they weren't a danger to us in general.

"Yes, we'll find a way." And for once, I almost believed it.

Next in the Splintered Magic Series

vinci-books.com/splintereddestiny

Brigid has realized it's time to stop playing defense and begin the final battle for peace.

Vampires seek to seize Brigid's territory, while suspicious griffins threaten to uncover a promise-bound secret. Brigid must rally her elemental powers and loyal friends to take the fight to her enemies. As the lines blur between predator and prey, Brigid's resolve is unwavering—she will reclaim what's rightfully hers, even if it means unleashing the full might of her magical abilities and letting her cat handle the rest.

Turn the page for a free preview…

Splintered Destiny: Chapter One

Gabe was acting strange. He paced, he looked nervous, and he kept trying to talk, but repeatedly stopped after a word or two. I didn't know what was wrong.

"I know both of us had bad marriages," he started.

My heart sank and I felt sick. Was he breaking up with me? Did he choose this vacation as a way to say, "Your life is too crazy, I'm out?"

I was already dressed for dinner, but my ankles weren't going to hold me up in these shoes with the gut punch that was coming. After having one relationship come to a shocking end, I expected the worst. I didn't know if I would survive him leaving me. I sat heavily on the edge of the bed and breathed quickly then held my breath and focused on keeping it together—showing dignity. I gripped the bedspread so tightly my hands ached.

"I wish that I'd been smart enough to track you down earlier." Gabe pulled his shirt collar away from his throat. I could see the stress in his tight movements.

Maybe I was wrong. I let my breath go and took a few

deep, cleansing ones. I released the death grip on the bedspread. Maybe he wasn't breaking up with me. That meant... My heart raced. My palms started to sweat. Was he...?

"I didn't think I'd ever want to try again, but if you're willing, there just isn't anyone else for me."

My breath caught in my throat. My hand moved of its own volition to cover my mouth. My heart began to flutter in my chest. I was either having a heart attack or an extreme case of the butterflies.

His hand shook as he pulled out the small box from his jeans pocket.

I was glad I was sitting because I felt weak, and I knew my legs wouldn't hold me. I swallowed, my throat suddenly dry.

He knelt and handed me the open box. "Brigid Donovan, will you marry me?"

He looked straight at me. His heart shined in his hazel eyes, the candlelight gleaming off the moisture filling them.

My hand shook, but I reached down and took the box, my eyes never leaving his. I swallowed the lump that was closing off my throat. We'd been through so much together, and the love I felt for him was big. Bigger than I was. I couldn't even contain it in my body—it spilled out like the uncontrolled tears now running down my face.

I blinked them away and stared at the ring, glittering against the black velvet lining of the box. The ring was perfect. It wasn't a diamond, thank heavens. Gabe knew better. He knew I had weird superstitious feelings about diamonds—especially after my first marriage and the issues with my ice magic. It was hard to get over being beaten, having the magic taken from me, and only getting it back after several murder attempts. The ongoing battles over it with Sofia made me a little weird about diamonds. The ring sparkled in the candlelight. It was a large, round cut sapphire surrounded by white gold and intricate filigree. It was exquisite and perfectly me.

"Yes!" I sobbed.

I threw my arms around his neck while still holding the box. He stood up, pulled me off my feet, and kissed me soundly. He twirled us around, my hair flowing around my head like the dress's skirt floated around my knees as we both laughed and cried together. Once he put me down, he plucked the ring out of the box and placed it on my finger. I admired it for a moment and then kissed him again. The smile hurt my cheeks as the tears fell.

"I wish I'd done this when we were eighteen; it would have saved us both a bunch of heartache," he said.

"We couldn't have known, but I agree."

He nodded and looked down at his watch, "Are you ready to go?"

I wiped my cheeks. "Just give me a moment." I hurried to the bathroom and cleaned up my smeared mascara. I felt like skipping and would have if my feet ever touched the ground again. I walked out, smiled, and held up my ring-bedecked hand. "All fancied up and ready to roll!"

He grinned, the tension disappearing from his shoulders, and grasped my hand to stare at the ring. Then he pulled me in for another hug and kiss.

We were on vacation, just the two of us. After all that had happened, we needed time away. At least, I needed it. After the last vampire attack, I'd closed the inn. It was too dangerous for my patrons, and the house had been damaged. Gabe found us a lovely resort to escape to in Riviera Maya, Mexico.

Mr. Mittens was holding down the fort back home,

although he'd protested mightily about us going where he couldn't protect me. I told him I was a realm walk away and could be home at the first sign of any trouble. That *hadn't* mollified him. I had to promise to call Megan every day and check in. He'd have demanded I call him directly if he had pockets for a phone.

It was hard to leave him behind, but I needed to get away. I needed time with Gabe, and I needed to remember what it was like to be human—even if I wasn't. I had to let the stress go, or my magic wouldn't be the only thing acting wacky in my life. Since Dana had unblocked my magic, it was unstable but *stronger*.

Gabe took me to a fancy restaurant. It was in the resort, so it wasn't authentic Mexican food, but good food was good food. We'd been here two days.

I was excited about the proposal and unbelievably happy. My face ached from smiling, and having alone time with Gabe was everything. Still, in the back of my mind, I had to keep telling myself to relax, enjoy, and soak in the love.

I *tried* to be normal. I really did. I'd put on my game face and acted happy as hard as I could. We ate, we swam, we danced, we made love. I should be enjoying Gabe, the proposal, our time alone, but I still couldn't relax.

I didn't think I ever would until the vampires were gone and the griffins had been dealt with.

Gabe gave it a good try—ignoring my agitation—until he finally said, "Look, I know you can't stop thinking about everything. Let's just go home."

I felt terrible. He'd planned such a wonderful time and loved me so much. I loved him and wanted him to be happy as well.

His decision only added to my stress. I was mucking up

everything—my life, my business, my relationship. Even my cat was affected. The worst thing? I had *no* answers. I couldn't fix *anything*; I had no idea how to stop the vampires or mollify the griffins. But what really bothered me was I needed to take care of it fast before it came back to bite us all. Until then, I felt guilty having the time of my life. We packed up our stuff, and rather than take the plane home—my dumb idea to feel normal on the way here—I realm walked us back.

Mr. Mittens was happy, but I wasn't sure about anyone else. They were all in a holding pattern, waiting for me to either reopen the B&B or fire them all. That was another layer of stress. I wanted the B&B to flourish. I planned to reopen, and firing my staff wouldn't help in the long run. I'd have to start over—again. Plus, they relied on me for a job, for pay, and in the case of Jim and Chef Jack, for housing as well. When I thought of it, I started to hyper-ventilate.

Since the last attack two weeks earlier, no one had seen or heard from a single vampire or griffin. My staff kept looking at me sideways, trying to guess my next steps. In truth, if I were fully human, I'd probably need blood pressure medication. I might be independently wealthy, but at some point, I'd need an income to support it all. The B&B was my answer. I just needed it to be a functional business again.

Sorcha, my baincapall friend from Faerie, had added four more to her patrol. At least they didn't care if I reopened or not. It was easier protecting fewer people. Mr. Mittens didn't care about the inn, although he cared about its people, mainly me—and Megan, by default. He hadn't said much about Gabe, but I think he was keeping an eye on him, trying to determine if he was safe and good for me. That's the sense I got, anyway.

Once I gathered Megan and Mr. Mittens together, I sprang the news on them. "We're engaged!"

Hmpf, was Mr. Mittens' response, and then satisfied I was home, he wandered away to do his own stuff. I expected more from him. He was acting weird. Maybe there was jealousy?

Megan's response was more normal. She shrieked so loud, I jumped, and ran at me, holding out her hands in the "gimme" position. "Congratulations! That's magnificent! Let me see the ring." Then she dove for my hand aggressively.

I held it out, beaming, for her inspection.

"Wowzer, that's some rock! I love the sapphire, it's *so* you."

"I know. It's perfect; Gabe is perfect."

"Tell me everything, leave no detail out."

"Uh, everything?"

She rocked her hand back and forth. "If you must edit…I guess I'll live."

I laughed and told her about how nervous he had been and that I thought he was like that because he was trying to break up.

"No way."

"Yes, way."

"That boy adores you. He wouldn't break up!" she insisted.

"Well, my life is crazy. He's been kidnapped twice because of me and had to fight vampires. I wouldn't blame *anyone* for running as far away from me as possible."

"That's Evan messing with your mind."

"What? No. I don't think about Evan," I said.

"Because he messed you up. So, stop. Gabe isn't Evan, and he wouldn't leave you."

I looked her in the eye. She was deadly serious. Her surety helped settle my tension a micro amount. She could be right. I didn't have great judgment, or at least judgment I trusted, and I knew that was a result of the emotional abuse. There was also that pesky fact that Evan had dumped me for his pregnant girlfriend, which didn't help my trust issues.

"You are probably right. I am a bit of a mess. Thanks, I couldn't pinpoint why I've been so…" I shrugged. I couldn't think of the words.

"Stupid?" Megan supplied, smiling.

I laughed. "Yeah, perfect answer."

"So, is he moving in?"

"Yeah, he has the time off now since we were supposed to be gone longer. He went home to start packing. I'm going to put my stuff away and clear some space for him."

"Want help?"

"Sure!"

She followed me into my bedroom, which was soon to be mine and Gabe's. I looked around. A momentary sense of trepidation overwhelmed me. Megan caught my expression.

"What's wrong?" she asked, alarmed.

"It's nothing." I shook my head and waved the question away.

"I know you; you can't get away with that."

"It's just a stupid selfish feeling. It'll pass."

"What is it?"

I sighed and felt a flush of embarrassment. "I just had a moment where I didn't want anything to change. This is my first space all on my own, and other than Mr. Mittens, I haven't had to share it for almost a year now."

She was quiet for a moment. "That's normal. At least, it's hard to combine your life with someone else's no matter how much you care for or love them. I know. You'll get over it once you adjust."

I smiled at her gratefully. "Yeah, I know. It *is* just an adjustment, and I'm happy. I told you it was dumb."

"Feelings aren't dumb. They just are. You're doing the right thing with the right person. It'll be great."

"OK, no more maudlin moments. Let's work!"

We started moving things around and making space. Of course, that's when the griffins decided to come back.

Splintered Destiny: Chapter Two

Mr. Mittens droll voice in my head was what alerted me. *Brigid, you have winged visitors.*

"Not bats?" I asked, worried it was vampires.

No, griffins. I'll warn Brightfeather.

"Thanks."

I looked up at Megan—I didn't know if that was a wide broadcast by my cat or just to me. She hadn't flinched, so I said, "We have incoming griffins."

She sighed. "I was enjoying the break from the crazy."

"Me too."

We hurried out the back. Sure enough, a contingent of griffins was landing in the parking lot. At least there weren't guest vehicles to get in the way. Their royal pains in the ass were with the usual entourage of courtiers. I didn't know what the griffins called them, but my time in the high court of Faerie had added a whole litany of new words to my vocabulary.

Thorn and his mate Firial, the king and queen, stepped forward once they saw me.

"Your Majesties," I said. "Welcome back. I'd like to thank you formally for your assistance with the vampires."

They gave me stiff nods in acknowledgement. However, I sincerely doubted they were here only to receive my thanks. This had to do with Brightfeather. I think they were suspicious. I didn't know if they guessed about the chicks, but they had to know something was going on, or they wouldn't keep coming back.

"I've summoned Brightfeather, if that is the purpose for your visit?"

It is. Our son's mate should attend us at our court. We will request her presence.

I was afraid of this. Brightfeather couldn't leave her chicks. If she didn't go, she'd be offending the royals, and they could demand her presence. A conundrum. I didn't see a way she could get around this without telling them about her babies.

I felt a pulse of magic, and Mr. Mittens appeared next to me on his usual perch on the railing of the back porch.

Brightfeather is flying in. The chicks are asleep, Mr. Mittens said.

"It's not good, Mr. Mittens," I said silently.

His head lowered. He liked Brightfeather, and he was an honorary uncle to the griffin chicks. He knew the stakes. We all did. He'd fight as hard as the rest of us if we had to.

I could hear the distant beats of griffin wings, and soon enough, a shadow brushed past us as Brightfeather back-winged into the narrow space left by the crowd of griffins.

She landed and bowed before the royals. *How may I serve you?*

The griffin royals gave no preamble. The queen stated, *As the mate of our only son, we require you to return and take up his royal duties.*

My heart sank, and a frisson of fear blasted through me. We hadn't thought of this possibility.

Brightfeather looked stunned. I didn't think she'd thought of this possibility either. She knew they'd want to take the babies, but not her. Either scenario was a disaster. She threw a glance my way. Pure panic burned in her eyes.

"If I may, Your Majesties, Brightfeather has been my main general in the fight against the vampires. Could I beg for her continued assistance for a short time?"

They looked at each other, Brightfeather's eager gaze on them. She still looked rough. Losing her mate, and then taking care of three growing and rambunctious chicks was taking a toll.

They must have been communicating silently to each other, because Thorn spoke. *We will give you one month. Then, you must return.*

Brighfeather bowed her head in submission. I could sense her growing panic. *I will comply,* she said. She had no choice. From what she'd told me, their word was law, and they enforced it with deadly effectiveness.

They nodded to her, and the whole group lifted off the ground in a single leap, the whoosh of their wings nearly flattening us. We watched from the porch until the griffins were nothing but dots in the sky.

What am I going to do? Brightfeather cried.

"We have a month. We'll come up with something. Until then, take care of those babies. We aren't going to let the king and queen take your babies from you." I looked her in the eye so she could see I meant it. My friends had become closer than family. I didn't want to lose any of them.

She took a deep shaky breath. *Thanks, Brigid. That helps.*

You're right. We have some breathing room to figure this out. She leapt high into the air and flew off towards her nest.

I looked at my cat. "Have you taken meat to them lately? She looks awful."

I have. I hunt for them every other day. His tone was disdainful, like how *dare* I ask.

"I wasn't trying to insult you; I was just worried about Brightfeather," I said, trying to soothe his hurt feelings. He must have forgiven me, because he gave me a head butt. "Come inside, I want to talk to you about something."

He jumped down and strolled into the kitchen with me. He sprang up on the old kitchen table. It had been in this house since it was built, and all my family that had lived in this house had used it. It was a huge, solid farm table, and I loved it.

Mr. Mittens gazed at me, patiently waiting to see what I was going to tell him.

"Gabe is moving in," I blurted out. I didn't know why it was hard to tell him, other than I wasn't sure if he approved.

He blinked once, slowly. *That is all?*

He hadn't reacted like I thought. My cat was keeping secrets. I sensed he knew before I did that Gabe was going to propose. I narrowed my eyes at him. "Yeah, why?"

He looked away and licked a patch of hair as though it was bothering him more than usual. It was one of his tells, he was nervous. He also sounded more smug than usual. *You acted like it was something earth shattering. I was expecting a new invasion by yet a third race of dangerous creatures from this planet.*

"I thought it was big news." My tone was a little snippy. Something was going on; I'd get to the bottom of it.

Congratulations. He jumped down and strolled into the

front, escaping before I could question him about his shifty behavior.

I followed, because I still wasn't finished with my project, and I didn't know when Gabe would show.

Does this require me to move my bed? he asked.

I cringed. I hadn't even thought about it. But with two adult people, his large cat bed smack in the middle of the bed would have to be moved. When Gabe stayed on other occasions, Mr. Mittens just disappeared. That would be harder now that Gabe was going to be here fulltime.

"Probably, but it doesn't have to go far, just to a different spot."

He gave me a cat nod and wandered off. I think I'd hurt his feelings. I looked on my phone to see what the largest bed I could order was. My current mattress was king size, and Mr. Mittens and I were fine. Gabe would be crowded if the cat bed remained. There was a bed called an Alaskan king. It was almost two feet longer and wider than the regular king. Nine feet square. It was a good thing I had an extremely large room. The sheets must be like tents. It could be delivered in a few days, so I ordered it with a smile. I wanted to surprise my cat.

Gabe already knew that Mr. Mittens and I were a package deal. Plus, he was grateful to the cat for protecting me. I smiled at this, then frowned as I thought about what was before us.

Mr. Mittens and I had decided to take the fight to the vampires, but even though it had been two weeks since that decision, we still didn't have a plan. The link to Faerie gave this land free energy which kept us powered up. We both needed it. But we had no way to take it with us.

I'd given the problem to Dana, my great-grandfather's mistress of magic, but even though she was a master at making portable magic, she hadn't come up with a solution either. I thought, naively, that she'd be able to make a portable magic ball we could tap into, but apparently it didn't work that way.

Vamps grew stronger as they aged. They lost their sensitivity to sunlight and could shapeshift into more dangerous forms. Most young vamps could turn into bats, but they were small and almost harmless alone. Although when they swarmed, it was terrifying. The ancient ones could turn into man-sized vampire bats—absolutely horrific creatures with boundless strength and very bad attitudes. We believed Vic had exhausted his supply of ancient vamps when he threw them at us the last time, and we'd removed Bella from that lineup.

I sighed, exhausted from thinking about it and worrying about it for so long. I needed that vacation I'd cut short. I'm sure Gabe did, too. I sat on my bed. I would just lay down for a second...

Splintered Destiny: Chapter Three

I woke up with Gabe shaking me gently.

"Sorry, Bridge, but Megan has something important to tell us."

I struggled up. Gabe gave me a hand. I couldn't believe how tired I was. Too much worry, too much stress.

"What's up?"

"I'm not sure, something to do with Goch, and well, let's go out and let her explain. I'm not sure I understand what she was saying."

I stretched and followed him out. She was standing on the back porch. Goch was in the parking lot—no squished vehicles. He'd finally learned to avoid them, I hoped.

"What's up?" I asked. "Gabe said you had something to tell us."

Megan danced around, her eyes twinkling like she was going to burst out of her skin. "This is exactly what we need; you have to hear this story!"

I was too tired for this. I looked between her and Goch.

The teenage dragon looked pleased with himself, so I gave him my attention. I sat down on the porch steps.

"Ok, Goch, tell Brigid what you told me," Megan commanded.

The dragon's eyes glowed golden with pleasure. He loved being helpful. *Megan said that you were looking for a way to keep your power filled away from this land.*

"Yes, for me and Mr. Mittens," I answered, confused.

Well, the dragons have a legend. His tail whipped back and forth, and I grew concerned he would break something. *Long ago, there was a golden collar that had a huge red stone on it. It was said it could harness energy and be manipulated by the dragon wearing the collar. That's the way we'll be able to beat the vampires! We'll get the collar, and then you'll have access to your power wherever we go!*

I shook my head. My dragon charge was enthusiastic and willing to do almost anything for us, even letting us ride him when we needed a lift to Faerie, but this sounded too much like the other type of fairy tale.

"Goch, do you know if the collar really exists? It could just be a myth or legend." I wanted to let him down easily.

It's not a myth. I've seen it! I know where it is!

I looked at Gabe. He seemed as mystified as me.

"Just listen," Megan said. "Let him finish, you'll understand!"

"Where? When?" I asked Goch.

When I was a hatchling. My mother took me to the elders. She wanted their blessings for me. She talked to them while I waited. I wandered off and got lost in the caves. I wandered for a long time, and in one of the deep spaces, I saw it. A great golden collar with a large red gem. It was in the elder's hoard.

"Their hoard? Won't they be loath to part with it?" I asked.

I don't know. If it will help me and my friends and we bring it back, why would they mind?

I sighed. The sweet dragon was a bit naïve. But it was interesting. And an option we hadn't had before.

"Megan, is there any guarantee this collar will do what we want it to do?" I asked quietly so Goch wouldn't hear. He seemed so happy to have an idea.

"Nope. But it exists. That's a chance, and it's not like we have any other ideas."

She had me there. I looked at Gabe. "What do you think?"

He shrugged. "I think if we want to take the fight to the vamps, and not be sitting here waiting for them to destroy us, we should check it out."

I nodded. It seemed I was outvoted. Plus, there was the tiny spark of hope flaring to life in my belly. Maybe this was the answer.

"Ok, Goch. Tell us all you know."

His tail swished again, and his eyes lit up. *The stories say the gem can hold as much magic as you can fill it with. Dragon mages have a lot of power. It has to be able to help you and Mr. Mittens! There's a story that my mother told me when I was young. About how the collar was used to save the dragons long ago. There was this human mage, I think his name was Merson...*

"Merlin?" Megan interrupted.

Yes, that's right! Do you know him?

We looked at each other and laughed. "We've heard stories about him. He's probably the most famous earth mage."

Oh! He seemed deflated. Then perked back up. *He helped make the collar for the dragons! I think he called it an amerset? I don't know the word in English.*

"Amulet?"

Yes, that's it!

I was growing more and more excited. An amulet created by Merlin? Could it be the real deal?

"And you're sure we can borrow it?"

He paused. *No, I'm not sure, but it's important. So, they have to let us, right?*

"I don't think so, Goch, but we'll ask."

I'm a dragon, so I don't think it will be a big deal.

I laughed at his use of "big deal." He'd been hanging with us for so long, he'd picked up everyday usage in the language. It was cute.

However, I believed it would be a "big deal" to the dragons. An amulet created by Merlin? It sounded like a highly guarded treasure. Still, what choice did we have if we were to defeat the vampires?

I looked at Gabe, Megan, and Goch. I guess this motley crew was going on a quest.

Grab your copy...
vinci-books.com/splintereddestiny

About the Author

Jilleen Dolbeare writes urban fantasy and paranormal women's fiction. She loves stories with strong women, adventure, and humor, with a side helping of myth and folklore.

While living in the Arctic, she learned to keep her stakes sharp for the 67 days of night. She talks to the ravens that follow her when she takes long walks with her cats in their stroller, and she's learned how to keep the wolves at bay.

Jilleen lives with her husband and two hungry cats in Alaska where she also discovered her love and admiration of the Alaska Native peoples and their folklore.